More Trouble in Loveland

USA TODAY BESTSELLING AUTHOR

JENNIFER PEEL

To all the troublemakers in my life.
You know who you are.

One

"DON'T EVEN GET ME GOING on his breath," the woman told Dr. Mallard. Then she turned to her husband. "Why can't you brush your teeth at night? Is that too much to ask?"

Her husband looked up from his dress shoes. His eyes said *why am I here?* He sat as far away from her as possible, hugging the arm of the couch. It wasn't a good sign.

Dr. Ginny Mallard, whom I was shadowing, was at a loss for words. The wife had spent the last forty minutes of this session unloading on her husband. Did she ever have a laundry list— everything from his lack of help around the house to their lackluster sex life. And who could forget her diatribe about how he wasn't ambitious enough? She couldn't understand why, at thirty, he wasn't making at least six figures. Unrealistic expectations, anyone?

The husband hardly offered a word the whole session, not even in his defense.

I wanted to whisper to Dr. Mallard that the situation was putting the husband in an unfair position. She should have never given the wife so much time. But what did I know? I was only a student in my practicum. And Dr. Mallard hated students.

I had to do something. Technically, I was allowed to speak. Or at least, I was supposed to be able to. Dr. Mallard had basically told me to keep my mouth shut before the session started. But if there was any hope for this couple, the husband needed a reason to try, and the wife, who'd dragged him there, must want to save the marriage. Right? She was the one who asked— or probably more like demanded— they attend couple's counseling.

I took a deep breath and went for it. "Danica, tell us about your first date."

Dr. Mallard's head whipped my way. Her icy stare tried to intimidate me, but she had nothing on my husband's ex-wife. I didn't even flinch.

I faced the couple in crisis and waited for Danica's reply. She was taken aback by the request. I remember feeling the same way once upon a time when I was asked the same question, by my favorite teacher and mentor, Professor Yost. One of the best days of my life.

Jake, the husband, became mildly interested, looked at his wife, and waited for her to say something. Curiosity, and maybe fear, played in his worn eyes.

Danica ran her fingers through her luxurious blonde hair and thought for a moment. But as soon as her gray eyes narrowed and face tightened, my hopes for ending this session on a good note went out the small window in the office.

Danica let out a disgusted breath before she let it all out. "It was every girl's dream date." Sarcasm clung to every word.

Jake's brooding brown eyes hit his shoes.

"First, he was an hour late picking me up. We missed our dinner reservation, so we grabbed a pizza, and he drove me up to the mountains for a picnic instead."

Sounded like my kind of date.

"Of course, it started to rain." Danica was a downer.

That would have been excellent news for me. Dancing in the rain, or making out in the rain, or both at the same time— because we were talented like that— were some of my favorite things to do with Ryan.

"And to top it all off, he called me Leah when he dropped me off."

Ouch.

That perked Jake up. His head turned toward her, a sinister smile playing on his lips. Oh, that couldn't be good.

Yep, he snapped. Jake sat up, and it was like an imaginary hose had filled him with spite. Not that I could blame the guy, but after his forthcoming confession I could confidently say there were bigger reasons this marriage wasn't working. I was sure this would be their last marriage counseling session. They were headed for divorce court.

"Leah," he said her name like I would say Ryan's. "I should have married her instead of you."

The fire in Danica's eyes was unquenchable, and it shot out at everyone in the room. "That's my sister you're talking about, you—"

"Tell me something I don't know," Jake interrupted. His stare was scathing. "No, let me tell you something."

Then he pulled the pin out of his grenade. "Leah and I are sleeping together."

In that moment, all the air was sucked out of the room in a silent but deadly blow.

Not even Danica uttered a word, but tears filled her eyes. Maybe a hint of remorse glimmered in Jake's, but I mostly saw relief.

When Danica came to, she grabbed her bag and left, slamming the door on her way out.

Dr. Mallard and I focused on Jake, who shrugged. "It was a mistake to marry the hot sister."

As a professional in training I had to keep from wrinkling my nose at his distasteful comment.

Jake proceeded to unload three years of misery and told how he had fallen in love with Leah, the cute but sweet sister who idolized him.

The upcoming holidays were not going to be fun in that family.

Dr. Mallard gave Jake a homework assignment to read a book about how to save a marriage in crisis. His smirk said he wasn't going to read it. I was surprised she recommended it. Professor Yost said that was a sign of an unskilled counselor. She needed to be recommending divorce counseling. It was apparent Jake had no interest in saving his marriage, which was probably dead on arrival. But I sat like a good student again and took notes.

Once Jake left and it was time to fill out the paper-work, I got an earful from Dr. Mallard. I knew I would. I was in favor of a client-centered approach, and obviously she didn't like adapting during a session.

"Why would you ask such a ridiculous question? Did you see what happened?" Her beady, dark eyes bore into me.

I stood my ground, or at least sat up tall in the uncomfortable, high-back chair I was sitting in. "My professor—"

Dr. Mallard rolled her eyes. "This is why I dislike dealing with students. Your professors aren't living in the real world. They preach from glass towers."

"Professor Yost was a practicing therapist for several years."

That shut her down, at least for the moment.

"He believed a good way to tell if a couple had a chance in therapy was to ask them about a time like a first date or the wedding day so he could gauge how they remembered it and what stuck with them. Danica was obviously resentful, and I would say she never felt confident or comfortable in their marriage. And her behavior reflected her discontent and unease."

Dr. Mallard stood up in clothes that screamed she hadn't been shopping since 1985. Who still wore shoulder pads? "You have a lot to learn, and, thanks to you, the divorce rate will be holding steady. Don't forget to fill out the paperwork."

I let out a huge breath when she left. Why was I paired with her today? My last day of my practicum for the semester, and it had to be with her. All the other counselors and psychologists at the clinic loved me.

Before I finished up the case and psychotherapy notes, I pulled out my phone and called my favorite number. "I love you." I didn't even let him say hello.

"Rough sessions today?"

"How did you know?"

"Because I know you."

The butterflies in my stomach still erupted when he talked to me like that. Some of them had been on a 24/7 bender ever since we were married six months ago.

"I could move some meetings around and come have lunch with you," Ryan offered.

"Sounds perfect, but I have my last study group in an hour. I can't wait until finals are over at the end of this week. And then we get Josh all to ourselves for two weeks. It's going to be perfect."

"Even with all the wedding chaos?"

"Thanks for reminding me." My dad and Felicity were finally getting married on Christmas Eve. Their love affair had been a series of ups and downs. They had planned on getting married in May, but they broke up in April, only to rekindle in June at my surprise wedding. Summer was mostly good for them. The beginning of fall was iffy, but supposedly this was a done deal. I wasn't so sure, but I was trying to keep my personal and semi-professional feelings out of it. I loved Felicity. I loved my dad. But they had more trouble in Loveland than most couples, as my dad liked to say. Not unlike Danica and Jake, my dad and Felicity had insecurities too. Unfortunately, a lot of them were fueled by Felicity's mom. That dear needed to get a new hobby and stop bashing my dad. But I couldn't think about it right now. I had finals, a husband who adored me, and a stepson I loved to pieces.

"I'm sorry. Take a breath, Charlee. I love you. And if

you aren't too tired tonight after Josh's Christmas concert, I'll show you exactly how much."

The butterflies were now swearing. "I'll do my best. Sorry I've been so exhausted lately, you know it's not you, right?"

"I've been wondering," he teased. "I know you've had a lot on your plate lately."

My schedule had been insane. Between school, practicum, wedding, Ryan, Josh, Victoria (Ryan's ex-wife), my best friend Krissy and her baby Taylar Ann (Krissy reneged on naming the baby after me. She went with her mom instead. What could I say to that?), I was wiped out. I fell asleep every night as soon as my head hit the pillow. I was being a pitiful newlywed, which was a shame because I loved every part of Ryan, and he was a rock star in the bedroom. "You're always my main course."

"I love it when you talk dirty to me like that."

I laughed. "I love you. I'll see you tonight."

"You have no idea how much I look forward to it."

Believe me, I did.

Two

I WASN'T SURE IF I couldn't eat because I was upset about the session with Dr. Mallard or if I was coming down with something. I was afraid it was the latter. I was having bouts of nausea, and my appetite was sunk. I shouldn't be surprised. School, mine and Josh's, was like a breeding ground for germs. Poor Josh had already been infected with strep throat and hand, foot, and mouth disease this school year. I hated when my big guy was sick, except it meant he would cuddle with me on the couch.

I held my abdomen on the drive to campus. I needed someone to cuddle with me. I wasn't feeling all that hot. The timing couldn't have been worse. I didn't have time to be sick. Thankfully, I wasn't working anymore. Ryan and I had decided my focus should be school and Josh. Ryan made more than enough to support us as a partner in my dad's accounting firm, and we both wanted me to get through school so we could give Josh some siblings. I wanted nothing more than to have a baby with Ryan, but I had a semester left of schooling, plus a year internship to finish my master's in counseling to become a licensed professional counselor. Professor Yost had suggested that route instead of a master's degree in psychology. He thought I had a knack for it and that it would bring me more fulfillment. He was right. I'm glad I didn't drop out of his class when he embarrassed me with a mock counseling session with Ryan at the beginning of the year; he had been a terrific mentor.

A few times I'd almost told Ryan we should just get down and start making that baby, but then I'd babysit Taylar Ann for Krissy, and that thought went right out the window. You had to keep your eye on those little things at all times. It's like they're hardwired to want to injure themselves. So we would wait one more year and then try. In the meantime, we would practice. Well, hopefully. Where had all my energy suddenly gone?

Mind over matter, mind over matter. I thought internally chanting this would help. Nope. I still felt like crap. Maybe it was nerves about finals and a vitamin deficiency. Anything but an illness.

I did my best to push through and met with my study group in the library. Our psychopathology exam was on Wednesday, and it was the toughest, best class I had taken that semester. It had given me such a good perspective about how all aspects, from biological, political, social, cultural, and psychological forces, define who we are. The professor was tough, but fair. Her term exams were brutal, and I didn't expect this final to be any different. My guess was that it would be worse.

I took a page out of Ryan's book for studying for exams and made flashcards for my group. Everyone loved me. They especially loved my smart-aleck cards like, *What is the average number of nostril flares per class?* Our professor was famous for her expressive nose. The answer was fifteen.

Our group was made up of seven people from diverse backgrounds. There was even a grandmother in our group, Penny. She had pink hair, and I adored her. I told Ryan when I turned sixty-five I was going pink, maybe blue. For some reason that didn't surprise him. Probably because I had made him dress up as the Spartan cheerleaders from Saturday Night Live for Halloween this year. Or that I had made him jump on our trampoline in our wedding clothes after we tied the knot in our backyard. It was a tossup. I liked keeping him on his toes. And I loved that look he gave me that said, "What am I going to do with you, and why did I let you talk me into this?" I knew why. He loved me, plain and simple, even if I drove him crazy on occasion.

I did my best to stay alert and offer anything valuable to the discussion during the two-hour study group that felt more like ten, but I found myself leaning on my hand more often than not and yawning uncontrollably, all while feeling like I wanted to puke. And not the good kind, like the kind the butterflies made me feel around Ryan. I couldn't even pay attention to the obvious budding romance between the woman in our group that was addicted to teeth whiteners and the beanpole guy with the deepest voice ever that fawned over her and clapped when she got the answers right.

My lack of participation didn't go unnoticed. Penny

caught up to me on my way down the hall afterward in her bright joggers and neon shoes. "Hey there, missy. You feeling okay? You're normally the life of the party."

I shifted my book bag around my shoulder. It took more effort than it should have. "I think I picked up something from Josh." Everyone knew who that was. I talked about the kid incessantly and wore his noodle necklaces often. I had gotten an upgrade, and he'd made me one with chunky wooden beads he'd hand-painted at preschool. I would be wearing it proudly tonight at his concert.

Penny nudged me with her bony elbow. She hardly had any meat on her. Probably because she ran circles around everyone. "Are you sure you didn't pick up anything from your husband?" She nudged me a few more times. "You know what I mean?" She wagged her eyebrows.

I stopped, confused. Ryan was never sick. "What do you mean?"

"Do you need a lesson about the birds and the bees?"

"Uh. No. I think I have that particular lesson down and memorized."

Penny's eyes lit up. "That's exactly my point."

I tilted my head.

"I know you're not this dense."

Now not only did I feel ill, I felt incompetent. "Um…"

"Are you pregnant?" The little old lady's voice carried through the crowded hall, making everyone stop and stare at me.

Penny's audacity and words bounced around in my head. I stood stunned. It took me a second to come to.

"No." What a ridiculous question, and it wasn't any of her business. I began to walk away through the crowd of people still gaping at me. I gave them all my best "nothing to see here" look.

Penny didn't get the hint and chased after me. She was spry for her age. She strung her arm through mine. "Listen, there is no tired like pregnant tired, and you have a sudden glow about you."

"It's a green glow from being sick to my stomach."

She laughed. "Yep, you have all the signs."

I wasn't pregnant. We used birth control religiously. It was like a commandment in our home right now. Thou shalt always use contraception. "I'm sure whatever virus I have will pass over soon."

Her cackle was a mix of amusement with a hint of "you're so naïve." "In about eight to nine months. But then the real fun begins."

I wriggled out of her clutches. "I'm running late. I need to get going."

"I bet you're late." She cackled again.

Late? Was *I late?* When I reached the privacy of my car I pulled out my phone. I had a handy app that tracked all my lady things. I clicked on it and, sure enough, I was three days late. Hmmm. That wasn't completely abnormal. I'd been late before due to stress, and if ever I was stressed, now was the time. Between school, home, the wedding, and the holidays, my life was in a perpetual state of chaos. I took a deep breath. I couldn't be pregnant, could I? That thought played in my head while I sat there in my cold car in a paralyzed state.

It's not like it would be the end of the world. In fact, I knew Ryan would be thrilled. He'd been ready to have a baby since we said, "I do." Or more like when I shouted "yes"— I'd been a tad excited that I was marrying the man I had been head over heels for since I was fourteen. I had fantasized about that day for twelve years. We had taken the long way around getting there, but I had guessed since he was twenty-two when I was fourteen that it made sense. And even though I knew when I was seventeen he was marrying the wrong woman, I was now glad that he had. We got Josh out of that deal, and I couldn't imagine my life without that kid. I *could* imagine life without his mother some days. She had that "I just ate peed-on-Cheerios" look down and gave it to me frequently. I knew I was in for some of those looks tonight at Josh's pre-school concert, where we all would be. I thought maybe since she was now dating her hoity-toity French boyfriend, Maxime, she would be more pleasant. But no, he had the peed-on-Cheerios look down too.

Maxime was the reason we were getting Josh to ourselves for two whole weeks. He was whisking Victoria away for a European holiday. Maxime was only living here through next year, when his season as guest conductor of the orchestra in Denver was over. Neither Ryan nor I was surprised Victoria ended up with someone like Maxime. He was duller than dull, but he thought highly of himself. You only had to ask him. He name-dropped like you wouldn't believe. The funny part was the names he was dropping were mostly unknown to Ryan and me. We didn't really keep up on the world of symphonies, orchestras, and composers. Now, ask us about any professional football or basketball team, and we could talk shop.

The sad part was, I didn't think Maxime was kid friendly. He was disinterested in Josh, and Victoria usually only saw Maxime when Josh stayed with us. Ryan and I were both concerned about it. And Ryan had already warned Victoria he wouldn't allow Josh to move out of state or country if Maxime and Victoria's relationship progressed the way it was looking like it could. The thought of Josh out of our zip code made me feel ill.

Speaking of feeling ill, I rubbed my hand against my abdomen.

No. I couldn't be. Could I?

Three

I LEANED MY HEAD ON Ryan's shoulder and laced my fingers with his. I wanted to close my eyes, but since we were surrounded by family, strangers, and frenemies, a.k.a. Victoria and her cronies, I forced myself to stay awake while we waited for Josh's concert to start in the gym of his preschool. I wasn't sure what was wrong with me. I was only twenty-six years old. I was in my prime.

Ryan kissed my head. "Are you okay? You were quiet on the drive over."

I thought about Penny's two cents. Pun intended. But I didn't want to mention it to Ryan. No use in getting him excited for no reason. And if on the off-chance I was, I wanted to tell Ryan in a memorable way. I was thinking as part of his Christmas present, which I still needed to buy. We decided we would only buy each other one thing this year, and it had to be meaningful and cost under a hundred dollars. We would be in Beaver Creek at a resort for seven glorious days, including Christmas. No need to haul a million gifts up there, except for Josh's. He had already checked to make sure Santa was going to know where we were at. And it wasn't like Ryan and I needed or wanted anything. Our first Christmas together would be memorable with or without gifts.

My dad and Felicity were getting married at the resort, and we were arriving a few days before the Christmas Eve nuptials and staying until a few days after Christmas. I couldn't wait to spend our days on the slopes with Josh and our nights cozied up together, minus Josh. Well, Josh would probably end up with us at some point. We woke up many nights to find him snuggled between us.

My head popped up. *Should pregnant women ski?* Maybe I should take a test, just to make sure.

Ryan's gorgeous green eyes questioned my sudden departure from his shoulder. "You never answered me. Are you okay?"

I leaned in and pecked him on the lips. It gave me a little energy boost. "Better now." It was sort of true. I still felt like crap, but kissing Ryan always made me feel better.

"Hey, now." My dad was making his way with Felicity through the crowd to the seats we had saved for them. "Just because I let you marry her doesn't mean I want to see you kissing my baby girl," he teased Ryan.

I went to stand up to hug both him and Felicity, but Dad gestured for me to stay seated. He leaned down and kissed my cheek. "You okay, honey?"

"Why does everyone keep asking me that?"

Dad looked between him and the lovely Felicity, who was wearing a simple red dress that suited her. Both Dad and Felicity shared a concerned look.

"You look tired, baby girl."

"Good, because I am."

"Are you keeping my daughter up too late?" Dad narrowed his eyes at Ryan before he really thought about what he was asking.

Felicity and I laughed when Dad had to back that train up.

"You know, I don't want to know."

Ryan looked relieved not to have to answer. It was always a delicate balance with Ryan being my dad's business partner, friend, and now son-in-law.

While Dad and Felicity settled next to us, Ryan took the moment to whisper in my ear, "I'm hoping to keep you up late tonight."

Erupting butterflies added to the nauseated feeling I already had going. My poor body didn't know how to feel. But when Ryan put his arm around me, it didn't matter how I felt physically. Loved conquered all. "Count on it." I tried to be covert. I also told my body who was boss— I didn't care how it felt, we were still in the honeymoon phase, and we were going to act like it. Maybe I could take a nap first. I sank against my husband.

The peace wasn't meant to last. Victoria, who was keeping a seat between her and Ryan empty like a child, decided she needed to speak. Beyond saying hi when we arrived, I had been doing my best to ignore her and the group that came with her.

Victoria's eyes tried to burn into me, but she addressed Ryan. "Do you know what Josh called Charlee today?"

"Cherry?" Ryan was confused by the ire. Josh, from day one, had called me Cherry. We knew it annoyed Victoria that he didn't use my "proper" name, but I thought we were past that.

Ryan and I both turned and faced her. She was still a raving, red-headed beauty who felt the need to dress to the nines no matter the occasion. Tonight, she wore a tight, silver sheen dress. She had her hair pulled up in a bun, giving her a severe but runway-model sort of look. I might have been jealous of her except she was in a perpetually bad mood, and if that's what being beyond gorgeous did to you, no thank you. I would have thought since she finally found love— because she never really loved Ryan, which was ridiculous on her part— she would at least smile. But then I looked at Maxime, who wore the same look of disdain. I was surprised to see him there. Like I said, he wasn't all that interested in Josh or the domestic life. Look at the man— he was wearing a burgundy ascot to a preschool performance, and he had his dark hair slicked back. All he needed was a smoking jacket and cigar to complete the Hugh Hefner look.

Maybe it was bad on my part, but I wanted to laugh at the pair. He was shorter than Victoria's five-feet-eleven stature, and when he put his arm around her he looked like a child in a grown-up suit.

"No. He called her 'Mom.'" Venom spewed out of her.

I put my hand on my heart. "Really?" Oooh, I probably shouldn't have said that, from the utter hatred in Victoria's eyes, but I was hoping one day we would trade in "Cherry" for "Mom." I mean, I was his stepmother, though I didn't like that title— it made me sound old and possibly wicked— and any siblings of his that Ryan and I brought to the table would call me Mom. But I had never brought it up or forced the issue. Regardless of how I felt about Victoria, I knew she was Josh's mom, and I wasn't looking to take her place. But I had been secretly reading several articles on my psychology boards about what stepparents should be called. There were numerous opinions, but most agreed it came down to the connection between the child and the stepparent and what made the child most comfortable.

Ryan looked between Victoria and me. It was a difficult place to be. His lip twitched like he wanted to smile, but he kept it under wraps. It was a balancing act for him. I placed my hand on his thigh to let him know I supported whatever may come out of his mouth. Ryan shrugged. "It makes sense."

That wasn't what Victoria wanted to hear. "I. Am. His. Mother." She pronounced every word with perfect diction, all while trying to keep her voice down. This really wasn't the venue for this discussion. It was garnering not only the attention of our friends and family, but the innocent bystanders all around us. But I mean, who didn't love a little drama at a preschool event?

My dad grabbed my hand for support while I watched Victoria's brother, Jonathan, and the wicked witch sister-in-law, Osanna, laser-focus in on me. Unfortunately, I was used to the glares. Maxime stared at his phone, disinterested as always.

Ryan took the chair right next to Victoria, trying to

keep the conversation private, though I could still hear every word. "And you're a good mother." Ryan was one of the most decent men I knew. After everything Victoria had put him through from being indifferent during their seven-year marriage to the divorce, he always showed her respect as the mother of his son. But that didn't mean he always agreed with her. "Josh calling Charlee 'Mom' doesn't take that away from you. I would hope," his eyes drifted toward Maxime, "if you decide to marry again, Josh would feel as loved by your husband as he does by Charlee. That's what this boils down to."

I could feel the waves of heat rolling off Victoria. If her narrowed eyes shot fire, I would have been toast. "She will never love him like I do."

"Maybe, but regardless, she does love him, and he loves her. If you would rather, he can call her 'goddess' instead. It's your choice." Ryan slid back next to me without another word.

I had to press my lips together to suppress the toothiest grin ever. The night Ryan asked me to marry him I told him I wasn't fond of the title "stepmother," and he had suggested "goddess." I never expected him or Josh to call me that, but never in a million years did I expect Ryan to tell Victoria about it.

Victoria's face matched her red hair. Her eyes tried to bore a hole in me. She kept opening her mouth to speak, but only *tsks* and tongue clucks escaped. It was a dilemma for her. Mom or goddess? She saw me as neither. To her I was still the teenager who had served punch at her and Ryan's wedding. Yeah, that sounded as weird as it was. I thought back to the purple grapefruit rollup dress she'd made me wear for it. I had torched that baby in honor of their unholy union. Like I said, I was glad we got Josh out the deal, but that day, it was apparent that Victoria didn't love Ryan.

"What are you smiling at?" Victoria found some words for me.

I had been thinking about when I burned that dress in my grandparents' fireplace. It was one of the worst times of my life. Not only had Ryan just gotten married, but my dad's affair had just come to light, and I was whisked away by my mom to Kansas, away from all I knew and loved in Colorado. Burning that dress was symbolic to me. I vowed never to think about Ryan from that time forward. And for almost eight years I hadn't. But when I moved back to Colorado a year and a half ago, all that changed. Ryan was divorced, and I realized my feelings for him had not changed. He, on the other hand, had to come to terms with the fact that the girl next door had grown up. We had our fair share of trouble while Ryan figured out his feelings and how to deal with Victoria when it came to me, but he got there.

I took my husband's hand and smiled at her. "I'm excited to see Josh sing."

That wasn't a lie. Mentioning the burning of the dress might have cost me my life, or at least caused a scene. And we had already given all the other parents plenty to talk about over the last year. For some reason Victoria could never school her emotions when she was around us. She never did anything crazy, but it was obvious she didn't like me. That dislike had only grown since we'd decided to get married. It's one of the reasons we had a "surprise" wedding. Besides, it was more fun that way. But I thought our relationship would have improved. I mean, she had apologized to me once upon a time for her behavior. But I think part of her thought Ryan and I wouldn't last. I think deep down she had been counting on it.

Victoria gave me one more vile look before turning to Maxime and her brother and sister-in-law. Jonathon and Osanna were trying to comfort her, and Maxime kept checking the time. I hoped Victoria knew what she was doing with him. I found it odd that Victoria would give up her Christmas with Josh to travel with Maxime. And why didn't she want to take Josh? Not like Ryan and I would have liked it, but Ryan had taken Josh to D.C. last year during Christmas to visit his parents. I had no love for Victoria, but she was a good mother. Maybe not a fun mom, but until recently, she had always put Josh first. Since things had heated up between her and the stiff Frenchman, we'd had Josh more often than normal. Definitely not complaining about that. But when Ryan and I were dating we'd included Josh. Ryan never gave up any of his days. Heck, I was tempted to take Josh on our honeymoon. The thought of being without him for a week killed me. Ryan talked me out of it. And it was a good call. A lot of adult activity happened that week in paradise, otherwise known as the Saint Lucia.

Oh, Saint Lucia, you and I and Ryan would get reacquainted someday. I rubbed my abdomen. Someday when I felt better and life wasn't so crazy. *Could I really be pregnant?*

There was no time to think about that. Though it had been playing in the back of my mind ever since Penny blurted it out. I leaned in closer to Ryan. *A baby? Maybe?*

Ryan kissed my head.

I tugged on the wooden bead necklace my favorite kid gave me. What would Josh think about having a brother or sister? I had to stop myself from getting excited by the idea. Nothing would make me happier than to add to our family, but the timing wasn't the best. But, then, when would it ever be?

The lights in the gym dimmed. It was finally time. Fifty preschoolers marched out in varying shades of red and green clothing, wearing big grins and reindeer antlers. Josh was so proud of his, he had worn them all last weekend while we had him. They jangled, too, so we always knew where he was. I got out my phone, along with every other parent, to take pictures and record the cuteness on the tackily decorated stage. I loved it. They had let the kids decorate, and it showed. There were strings of paper chains and oddly shaped snowflakes everywhere. It kind of reminded me of our tree at home. Josh thought he should be in charge of decorations, and we'd let him go to town. We were cleaning up paper and glitter for days. I was still finding glitter all over our house. But Josh was happy and proud of himself, and that's all that mattered.

Victoria had turned her nose up at it when she came to get him yesterday; she had him this week until Friday, when she left on her European holiday. I had seen her tree a couple of weeks ago when I picked up Josh. It was stunning: nine feet decked out in painted gold flowers and berries. Each gift under her tree looked professionally wrapped in gold and silver, with big, fancy bows to match. It was pretty enough for a department store window. The gifts we had under our tree were wrapped in patterned paper with Santa and snowmen. I counted myself ahead of the game for even having any gifts for Josh wrapped. There wasn't a bow or ribbon in sight. I figured he would be ripping them all to shreds anyway. And let's face it, I didn't have a decorator bone in my body. Ryan didn't seem to mind. Our house looked about the same as when it was Ryan's bachelor pad. I may have added a couple of throw pillows to the couch, and our framed wedding pictures, but other than that, not much had changed.

I think Victoria thought we weren't strict enough. We just looked at the haphazard tree like we were letting Josh be a kid. It's not like we were letting him run around with scissors or play with fire. But what harm was it to let him decorate the tree? It made me smile every time I looked at it because I remembered how happy it made Josh.

And there he was on stage waving and showing off his big goofy grin. He had just turned five and was getting so tall. He towered over the other kids. The kid came from some height. Victoria was keeping his red hair short, so no more curls, but dang if he wasn't the cutest kid up there. Even if his mom dressed him like he was attending one of Maxime's stuffy concerts. He was the only kid up there in a vest, with a red tie and black suit pants. He was styling but overdressed.

I snapped a bazillion pictures of him before he even stood on the risers. I was one of the annoying parents that stood up to make sure I got my kid in the photo. Victoria gave me the evil eye for it. But guaranteed she was going to ask me for a copy. I didn't wait. I texted her a copy of a few as soon as I sat down. I really did wish we could be friends. Or at least like one of those women you call your friends, but really you just see them once in a while and wave hi and smile. I wasn't sure if I'd ever seen her smile.

I caught a glimpse of Victoria picking up her phone to see my text. She gave no reaction other than to put it in her bag. I didn't expect a "thank you," but it would have been nice.

"Do you see how cute he is?" I gushed to Ryan, Felicity, and my dad. It was the most energetic I had felt all day.

"He's going to be the most darling ring bearer." Felicity agreed with my summation of him.

I only prayed the wedding was really going to happen this time. Especially since my dad had already sold his house for Felicity. He was moving out after their honeymoon. I had to hold back tears every time I drove by and saw the sold sign, which was every day, since we lived next door. I was still bummed about it, even if I understood why and agreed with his decision. I knew if Ryan and Victoria had lived together in our house, I would have been hesitant to live there, or maybe I would have refused to. But that was my childhood home. It's where I met Ryan for the first time and where Dad and I played basketball for hours on end in the driveway. Not to mention all the slumber and birthday parties.

But for Felicity, the house was my mother's ghost.

And I understood that. It wasn't until this summer that Dad had taken down all pictures with my mom in them. My mom was his first love, and they had built that house and a life together. And it was his selfish, stupid mistake that ended it all. It took him a long time to forgive himself. Longer to get over it, over her. Felicity had had a front row seat for it all. She wasn't ever sure there would be room for another woman in his life. Felicity's mother didn't help the situation by always reminding her about all the negatives, from how long it took him to propose to the all the break ups, and she especially hammered in that she would never have children of her own if she married Dad.

Dad was fifty-four now and had no desire to have more children. He loved being a grandpa to Josh and couldn't wait for me to have some more for him. He was in the time of his life where he wanted to travel and enjoy his success. He didn't want to be up in the middle of the night with crying babies.

Felicity knew all that when they started dating, and she was okay with it until several months ago. I guess at forty-three, her biological clock started ticking at a furious pace; or maybe her mother, Celia, had gotten to her. Celia thought it was a crying shame she was giving up her chance to have her own. Even my dad agreed. He didn't want Felicity to be unhappy or ever feel like she was missing out on something. He truly loved her. He told her in the spring if that's what she wanted, he would let her go.

Felicity took it as him saying, he didn't want her, so she quit her job at Jensen and Carter Accounting, and we didn't see her for several weeks. Dad was miserable, which made me feel guilty, because I was happier than I had ever been, engaged to Ryan. So when Ryan and I planned our secret wedding for the middle of June, I knew I needed to invite Felicity, even if it meant it would be awkward with my mom there.

We won't go into what my mom thought of Felicity or what she accused my dad of, but you could probably guess in light of his affair and the fact that Felicity was once his secretary. It wasn't true, but I probably would have asked the same question if I was in my mother's shoes. My mother was also unhappy that she didn't get to do all the "normal" things that mothers of the bride got to do, like dress shopping. I wore a simple, off-the-shoulder, white dress that I picked up in a department store, and I went barefoot. To me it was perfect.

Most everyone thought we were having a barbecue in Ryan's backyard to christen his new deck. Nope. I mean, we did have a barbecue and one fantastic party, but in between we tied the knot. It was just how I wanted it. No fuss, no personalized lip balm tubes, not even an announcement. No hooker heels or fittings. We didn't want gifts or showers and bachelor parties. We only wanted to celebrate our love with the people who meant the most to us. Even though that meant some of Ryan's friends from his days with Victoria came— Trixie was there. Who would have ever thought I would have had that dear at my wedding? But Alec, her husband, was one of Ryan's best friends. And we couldn't invite him without her. Believe me, I threw that idea out there.

Trixie texted Victoria the whole time she was at our place; it was probably the only reason she came. She was eager to get some dirt on me. And I know she thought she caught us being deceitful when, in the middle of the party, we announced we were getting married. (Best surprise ever, by the way.) I'd never seen fingers go so fast. Joke was on her. We'd told Victoria the day before. She was at least decent enough to keep it a secret. But I swore I saw her eyes water up when we mentioned we were tying the knot. I knew she didn't love Ryan, but I think she had hoped she would find love before him, because in her mind, all that was wrong with their marriage was him. Lots of unmet expectations for her. But honestly, I wasn't sure she knew how to be happy.

Now I worried about Felicity and my dad. Would they be happy? Dad was doing everything he could think of to show her how much he loved her and wanted to be with her, but would it be enough for Felicity or her mother? I looked over at the two of them. Dad held her hand. He was running his thumb across the large diamond he had bought for her last year when he'd proposed on Christmas Eve. She acted content, leaning against Dad, watching my big guy on stage. They were an attractive couple. My dad had that distinguished, gray-haired-man look. He had kept himself in shape and still dressed stylishly. Felicity had gorgeous, ice-blue eyes and wavy, dark brown hair that I knew she dyed, trying to fight off the gray. She was dainty compared to my dad, but they looked well together.

Let's hope they stayed together this time.

I placed my focus back where it should be, on the stage. The kids were all lined up now. It was a feat to wrangle three- to five-year-olds. Sometimes I had a hard time just getting Josh to do simple things, like brush his teeth. I couldn't imagine having fifty of them. But I could imagine a few more. I rubbed my stomach.

Josh was on the top row because of his height. I could see the excitement bursting from his beautiful green eyes that looked like his daddy's. I loved both sets more than I could say. I wouldn't mind if all our children inherited those babies. I would gift them my wit, since Ryan had none. He did try, and that was funny all on its own.

The first number of the night was "Rudolph the Red-Nosed Reindeer," hence the antlers. Josh had been singing that song on repeat for the last month. Sometimes he forgot some of the reindeer names, or he would say them wrong— like Blitzen was Blizzard. He wasn't mispro-nouncing words like he used to. I missed him calling spaghetti, psghetti. And he wasn't as snuggly as he used to be unless he was scared at night or sick. He was still willing to hug us in front of his friends, but absolutely no kissing. And he wanted to do everything himself, including combing his hair and picking out his clothes. Though I doubt he picked out what he was wearing tonight. Lately, all he wanted to wear was sports clothes, like jerseys and shorts, but it was too cold now. He said he hated wearing jeans because it took too long to get them up and down when he had to pee. Elastic was his friend. He killed me.

Josh sang loud and proud along with his friends and classmates. They did a few more numbers, including "Jingle Bells" and "Feliz Navidad." That was one song Josh mispronounced all over the place. At first I couldn't figure out why he was singing about a Felix Naughty Dog. When it finally dawned on me what he was singing I laughed so hard. Josh brought a lot of laughter and love into my life.

Could we be in store for more?

Four

"YOU WERE SO AMAZING!" I kissed Josh's cheeks that were no longer chubby. I didn't care that he didn't want me to in front of his friends. Good thing they were all busy being kissed by their families.

He gave me a quick hug before wriggling out of my arms. "Could you hear me?"

I stood up straight from kneeling at Josh's eye level. For a second all I could see were stars. Between that and the nausea, I grabbed Ryan's arm to steady myself.

Ryan intuitively held on and kept me upright. "What's wrong?" he whispered in my ear.

That was a good question. I'd never felt like this before, but this wasn't the time or place to discuss it. "I'm fine." I tried to reassure my husband.

He pressed his lips together. He wasn't buying it.

Josh grabbed our attention and repeated his unanswered question. "Did you guys hear me?"

Ryan high-fived Josh while he kept a hold of me. "Yeah, we did."

"You were the best."

Josh smiled like he agreed with my take on the situation. "Can we go get ice cream?" He gave us a big toothy grin. He knew how to work the system, but—

Victoria stood nearby. She had been the first to hug Josh after the performance. She had this amazing ability to grab our attention without saying a word, and with it she gave us her "don't even think about it" look. Not only was this her day to have him, but she was on this no-dairy, no-gluten, no-fat, no-carbs, basically no-taste diet. She was torturing Josh with it too. She tried to get us to adhere to it while he was with us. That was a no-go. We believed in liking what we ate. Maybe that's why she was so grumpy—she was hangry. Now if only I could convince her to have a cookie or something.

I let Ryan be the bearer of bad news. He ruffled Josh's hair. "We'll go this weekend."

Josh's mouth hung open wide. So maybe he was used to getting his way... a lot. The kid was seriously cute, and he had dimples. It's hard to say no to the dimples. Besides, he was a good kid, most of the time. He was still a kid, and he had his moments like all kids do. "Please, Mom?"

Oh my gosh. He just called me Mom. I was buying him a big-screen TV for his room, whatever he wanted. Tears filled my eyes while I dropped down and squeezed the life out of him. "I love you, big guy."

"Why are you crying?" Josh was confused.

I held his face in my hands. "Because I'm happy."

"So, does that mean we can have ice cream, tonight?"

We didn't have to answer this time. Victoria hovered over us. "It's time for us to go, honey." She wished me dead with her eyes. I had a feeling she heard Josh and didn't appreciate my tears of joy.

"Mommy, please?" Josh begged Victoria, but his eyes zeroed in on Maxime, who stood by Victoria's side looking like his skin was crawling from all us domesticated folk. In Josh's eyes I saw apprehension. I didn't like it one bit.

I stood up, and Ryan dutifully steadied me without any prompting. The stars came out again, but fewer this go around.

"Maxime," she said his name with a French flair, "and I made you some mango chia seed pudding."

That was every kid's dream. Right up there with Brussels sprouts.

Josh looked up at his dad in horror, begging him to save him from his fate.

Ryan put on a fake smile and lied through his teeth. "That sounds… good, buddy."

No one believed that, especially Josh. "Can I have some chocolate ice cream?" This kid owned my heart and taste buds. Not so much my taste buds now, since just talking about food was making me queasy. There was definitely something up. I loved food.

"No." Victoria nixed his request.

"Let's go, Victoria. We're late." Maxime tapped on his watch.

Late for what? Lame desserts?

Victoria took Josh's hand. "I'll drop him off at five, Friday morning."

Ryan and I both nodded. She had only told us her plans ten times. She had emailed us a detailed schedule—

almost hour by hour— of where she would be each leg of her trip. I still couldn't believe she was leaving Josh for two weeks. It didn't make her a bad mother, not at all, but it wasn't her.

Josh hugged Ryan and then me. It was awkward, since Victoria kept a hold of his hand. "Bye, Dad and Mom."

I was going to tear up every time he said that for a while. Even if it meant that I had to put up with Victoria's fire-breathing eyes. I didn't blame her for not liking it. Really, I didn't, but I wasn't going to tell him he couldn't call me that. That would only make him feel like his feelings were wrong. Ryan and I had been trying to teach him that feelings are natural and normal, but it's our actions we control. And couldn't the world always use some more love? That's all Josh was saying when he called me Mom. He wasn't saying I was his mother. I hoped Victoria got that. Her squinted blue eyes said she didn't. I hoped she didn't have a voodoo doll. Not that I could feel worse than I already did.

"We love you. See you Friday." I couldn't wait.

We watched the Victoria crony crowd walk off with the little love of our life. My dad and Felicity had had to exit as soon as the concert was over. They were hitting Felicity's company Christmas party tonight. Felicity was now working for a doctor's office as their office manager. Not sure if she would stay there once she and my dad were married. She wouldn't go back to being my dad and Ryan's secretary; that would be weird now. And they had already replaced her with Reginald. Best administrative assistant ever, according to Ryan. And guess what? Not only was

Reginald's name hoity-toity, but he had red hair. I teased Ryan about his obsession with redheads and uptight names. I didn't know he swung both ways with it. Ryan didn't find it as funny as me. And he reminded me he was partial to ash hair and women with male names, just like his wife. I loved when he called me his wife.

Ryan took my hand. "Ready to go?"

"Yep."

"Are you sure you're okay? I thought you were going to black out there, and you've hardly eaten anything the past few days. Are you coming down with something?"

"I think it's just stress?" Or maybe more, but again, no use in getting him all excited for no reason, or myself for that matter.

He led us off the stage. "You need to slow down. Maybe say no occasionally."

I thought about my huge to-do list and all the things I had said "yes" to. Tomorrow I was helping my dad pack up a few things before I finished a paper for one of my finals. And then I had to study. I had Felicity's wedding shower this weekend, and Krissy had asked me to help pass out gifts at the senior living center in town. Not to mention more exams and getting ready for our trip and the wedding.

"Do you really want me to start saying no tonight?" I played coy with my husband.

He kissed the side of my head. "You don't play fair, Mrs. Jensen-Carter." I loved that name. I had always planned on staying Charlee Jensen for my dad's sake since I was his only child, but for Ryan, I hyphenated.

35

"What fun would that be?"

His green eyes hit me as soon as we were out of earshot of all the innocent bystanders. Such passion lived in his eyes. "I'm ready for some fun tonight."

The butterflies overrode the icky feeling coursing through me and demanded that we play along and follow through. "Me too."

Ryan broke a half dozen traffic laws getting us home that night.

Five

I LOVED WAKING UP BEFORE him while lying in his arms. This way I could admire him without him knowing. I adored the way his light brown hair stuck up in several different directions and how his long eyelashes made the perfect half circle. I was amazed how much hair his face could grow each night while we slept. I loved how his lips were slightly upturned and seemed to smile even in his sleep. I liked to think it was me making him do so. I even loved the tiny nick on his chin where he had cut himself shaving a couple days ago.

The twinkling Christmas lights and light from the low-burning fire in our gas fireplace only enhanced his handsome face. I knew it was a genius idea to sleep under the Christmas tree. And this was one of our last opportunities before Josh came to stay with us.

His eyes opened as if he knew I was staring at him.

The butterflies in my stomach perked right up. Would he always cause such a reaction? I hoped so. After six months of marriage, the butterflies only seemed to be reproducing and adding new swear words to their vocabulary to express exactly how we felt about Ryan, so I think they were in for the long haul.

His sexy grin made an appearance. "Good morning, Beautiful."

I ran my finger down the side of his stubbled face before I leaned in to kiss him.

"Mmm." He crushed his lips against mine. "You fell asleep before my encore last night."

"Don't worry, the first two acts were standing ovation worthy." I snuggled against his bare chest under the comforter from our bed.

His fingers glided down my arm. "You up for running this morning?"

We were training for a half marathon in the spring. Don't ask me why. I mean, I knew why I was doing it— because I loved my husband, and he was excited about it. Not sure why he was excited about running 13.1 miles. I was only up to nine without dying.

The thought had me wanting to puke. I shook my head no against him.

"Is there something you want to tell me?"

"Like what?"

"Why you aren't acting like yourself."

"I'm just tired."

"You know you can tell me anything." He sounded worried.

"I know, and I do, but there's nothing to tell." I wondered if I would have something to tell him. I was going to buy a pregnancy test today if my period didn't start.

"All right. Try and take it easy today."

"I'll do my best." But I didn't see how that was possible.

"Do you want me to make breakfast?"

"No. I'll just eat some cereal or something." Anything cold. The thought of a hot breakfast was turning my stomach.

He gave me one more squeeze. "I'd better get up, if I can. I'm getting too old to sleep on the floor."

I mustered up a laugh. "You know it was fun."

"Very, but let's sleep in our bed tonight."

"Okay, old man. Go run."

I was going to soak in our garden tub to see if that would help.

He sat up and shook some pine needles out of his hair.

"That look works for you."

He reached down and picked some out of my hair. "You too. What do you think about Maxime and Victoria?" His tone went from playful to unsettled with his abrupt change of subject. He turned and rested his arms on his knees. His gaze stared off into the distance.

It took all the energy I had to sit up and lean my head against him. "I'm worried."

"Me too. I don't think he's good stepfather material."

"I agree, but what can we do if it goes that way?"

I felt his sigh. "I don't know."

"Have you tried to talk to Victoria about it?"

"It didn't go over well. She accused me of being jealous."

"Are you?" I teased.

His eyes roved over me in his dress shirt. "Charlee, I've never been happier in my life than when I'm with you. No other woman exists for me."

"Keep talking like that, and I'm going to demand an encore." I took his hand in mine, not sure I was up for an encore, and knowing I wasn't feeling good if thoughts of turning him down were running across my mind. "She knows the custody agreement won't let her move Josh out of state, and Josh is her life. And I don't see Maxime moving to Colorado, so maybe there's nothing to worry about."

"Maybe." He didn't sound convinced. "But I've never seen her behave like this."

"You know what it's like when you're first in love. You do stupid things, like telling your girlfriend you're not sure you want to be seen with her."

"Hey, I never said that."

"Close enough."

"We both agree I was an idiot, but this is different."

"How so?"

"She's always been independent. I've never seen her change herself to accommodate anyone. I can't believe she's leaving Josh for Christmas."

I thought for a second about how to comfort him. "What does your mom say? Don't borrow trouble. Let's just enjoy having him, and we'll cross any bridges over troubled water when and if we come to them."

He turned his head, his eyes locked with mine. "How did I get so lucky? And why do my shirts look better on you?"

I brushed his lips with my own. "You know why women started wearing men's shirts?"

His eyes said I amused him. "Why?"

"In the early days of movies, they couldn't show men and women sleeping together. As an alternative, they put women in men's shirts 'the morning after' even if they were married. But then it became a symbol of independence." We'd discussed this in my psychopathology class.

"I love you, Charlee. Life is never dull with you."

"I'm happy to hear that. Now, go run."

He leaned in and teased my lips with his. "How about an encore instead?"

My body said, uh. The butterflies told my body to get a grip. I let my lips answer for me. I closed the gap between us and made my husband late for work— again.

THE COLD AIR ON THE walk over to my dad's felt good. This was the strangest illness ever. I felt like I wanted to puke but couldn't. Along with this constant feeling of nausea, it felt like someone had hooked an industrial vacuum up to me and sucked all the energy out of me. I looked up my symptoms on some medical website after Ryan left for work, and I either had a terminal disease, the flu, a bun in the oven, or a massive case of PMS. Pregnancy was the best option in mind. If this was the new PMS, no thank you. It would be nice if our bodies could send our brains a message like, congratulations, you're not pregnant, or way to go, you've been fertilized. I guess I was going to have to pee on a stick.

I walked past the old basketball hoop and ran my fingers across the cold metal pole. Tears threatened to form. I don't know why I'd assumed my dad would live there forever and we would always be neighbors.

I looked around Mulberry Lane. Almost everyone's house was decorated for Christmas, even ours. Ryan had strung white lights around the house and on our pine trees. We'd also let Josh talk us into buying one of those tacky blowup snow globes for the front yard. We only plugged it in when he stayed with us. The Lawtons, Krissy's parents— my dad's other neighbors and my second parents, or more like third now, since I had Ryan's parents, who adored me— took the classy approach and decorated with real pine boughs and wreaths. Ann Lawton was a class act, plain and simple. She had four professionally decorated Christmas trees in her house, one specifically dedicated to her granddaughter, Taylar Ann. I'd never seen so many gifts. Taylar wasn't even old enough to open them by herself. But she was old enough to wreak havoc and pull every ornament within her reach off the trees. Things Ryan and I had to look forward to. Maybe?

I breathed in the cold air and waxed sentimental. I loved this neighborhood. I couldn't think of anywhere better to raise a family. It was a selfish thought, and one I would never admit to my dad, but I didn't want him to move. That basketball hoop was mine. And some single old man had bought the house. What was he going to do with it? What if he tore it down? That thought made me more ill. Ryan promised me we would install one in our drive come spring and that was great, but it wasn't the same.

I took one more look around before walking up the drive to the porch. No Christmas decorations this year. It was weird, but before I went in the house, it already felt empty. Maybe it was the stupid SOLD sign in the front yard. Or maybe I was hormonal. I was definitely tired. Ryan hadn't helped in that regard, but it was worth it. He always was.

I walked right into the sea of boxes and Saturday morning chore music. Not sure how to feel about that being played on a Tuesday, but you gotta love some Fleetwood Mac on any day. "Go Your Own Way" was blasting through the surround sound. It was fitting, I suppose. I was being dramatic. I mean, the man was only moving across town to a townhome off the lake. No more mowing the lawn for him. His new community was maintained by the homeowner's association. It was a beautiful place. Felicity had picked out everything, from the colors on the walls to the wood and granite; she'd even picked out every light fixture. They would be closing on it Friday and would move in when they got back from their honeymoon in Hawaii.

Dad was at the breakfast bar, per his usual, drinking coffee when I walked in, but he wasn't reading the paper. He had a stack of photo albums near him. He was so focused on the one he was looking at that he didn't even acknowledge my presence.

I stopped at the kitchen entrance and studied him.

Sniffles could be heard. It reminded me of a day long ago. The day that changed the course of my and my family's life forever. "Daddy," I called out like I was that seventeen-year-old girl.

He wiped his eyes before he would meet mine. "Baby girl, I didn't hear you come in." He closed the album as if closing a casket for the final time on a loved one.

I approached him and placed my hand over his on top of my parents' old wedding album. Tears filled my eyes too. "Taking a walk down memory lane?"

"Something like that. I want you to have all these. I probably should have given them to your mother, but they were all I had of you both for a long time."

Why did I feel like my heart was breaking? I was happy for my dad. And I had moved on from the past. I thought of one of the questions I would ask a patient who was having a hard time getting over past hurts and regrets. *What do I need in the present?* Or probably a better question in this situation, *what does my dad need?*

"I'll take good care of them," I promised. "But tell me what's going on."

He stood up and took his coffee cup to the sink to rinse it out. He was uncomfortable.

"Dad, you can talk to me."

His gaze was fixed on the window above the sink.

"Are you having second thoughts?"

"No."

"Then what?"

"I don't want to screw up again."

I took a deep, brave breath and asked a question that

filled me with dread. But I felt like I needed to ask. "Why did you in the first place?" I never understood why my dad had an affair. He was my idol, and when he fell, my whole world turned upside down.

Dad's turn to face me was like a slow-motion replay. "I wondered when you would ask."

His hazel eyes were more green; they got like that when he cried, which was a rare occasion. Last time I saw him cry was when I got married. He got his wish, and he was able to give me away. It's all he had wanted. And after everything he had done for me, I was happy to oblige. Though I think he was still upset we didn't let him pay for the wedding. There was nothing to pay for. Besides, Dad had paid for my tuition, and his wedding was costing a fortune. He was footing the bill. Just the cost of the suites and rooms at the resort were enough to feed a small country in Africa for a year. But Felicity's mother, Celia, insisted it was perfect and that her daughter only deserved the best. I think Felicity was embarrassed by it all, but my dad was trying to make everyone happy. It was an impossible task. But right now, my focus was on my dad.

Dad approached me with his hand held out. "Let's shoot hoops while we talk." We were two peas in a pod. Whenever we needed to think or work something out in our heads, we hit the court. Or when we wanted to avoid chores. Packing was a good task to delay.

I took his outstretched hand. The hand that brought me comfort and wiped away tears over the years. "I won't be much of an opponent today."

He pulled me in for a bear hug. "That's okay, I'll always be on your side."

That opened the floodgates. What was wrong with me? Why was I so weepy? I clung to my father, knowing our lives were about to take another drastic change. I would no longer be the number-one priority in his life. I knew that was how it should be; his wife deserved the honor.

"You'll always be my little girl." We were so in sync sometimes that I swore he could read my mind.

"I know. Now it's time to own you on the court."

He chuckled. "So cheeky."

"I thought we decided I was witty."

He wiped some of my tears away. "I was thinking more like perfect."

Six

I KNEW DAD WAS STALLING when he tried to see how many three-point shots he could make in a row. For fifty-four he still had it going on.

On shot ten I rebounded the ball and held on to it. "Dad."

He kicked an errant pebble on the driveway. "This isn't easy for your old man to talk about, especially with you."

"You don't have to." I did a bounce pass to him.

He easily caught the ball and made a shot. Nothing but net. This time he rebounded it and passed it to me. "I think it's time we had this talk. You're not going to charge me by the hour, are you?" He tried to add some levity to what was sure to be one of the most difficult conversations of my life.

"I'm not licensed yet." I took my shot and missed.

Dad tilted his head. "You really don't feel good, do you?"

"Just tired." It was a little white lie. More and more I was beginning to think I was pregnant, and as much as I loved my dad, that news was getting shared with my husband first.

Dad rebounded the ball in a stealth move. "You want to go inside?"

"The cold air feels good." That wasn't a lie.

"Why don't we play a game of H.O.R.S.E. while we talk," he suggested.

I nodded. "You go first."

He started off easy and took a shot from the free throw line. He focused on the basket instead of me. I suppose it was easier to confess that way. "At the time, your mom and I were having some issues."

"What kind?"

He made his shot and rebounded for me. "It was nothing major, but I was feeling underappreciated and think she was too."

"I don't remember you fighting."

Dad lobbed me the ball. "We probably should have. All too often I think we stayed silent, thinking issues would resolve on their own. But sometimes they festered."

"What kind of issues?" I prepared to take my shot.

"The usual suspects, money, time, sex." He was hesitant to throw that last one in there.

It was nothing new to me. This past semester I could hardly recall one couple counseling session I sat in where sex wasn't brought up. But when it's your parents, that's a whole other story. I took my shot, and the ball barely hobbled in. I was not at my finest. At least the cold was helping with the nausea. "I don't understand. You made a lot of money, and you and mom seemed happy."

48

Dad went out to the three-point line. "We were, for the most part. It was a hectic time of life. Business was booming, and it required a lot of my attention. Your mom felt alone, and sometimes I felt like I was only a paycheck to her. Physical and emotional connections were strained in the process."

Mom could shop like no one else I knew. She didn't get to as much now that she was married to Mark. He wasn't as successful as my father. Not even close. But Dad's statement made me think about my own actions in college, when we were barely speaking. "Did you think that's how I thought of you?"

He paused before he took his shot. A softness filled his features. "I was afraid, but deep in my heart, I knew there was more to the story, more to you. You are the least selfish person I know. And I blamed myself for whatever I thought may have become of you. I'm still kicking myself for not digging deeper."

"I probably wouldn't have told you." Even though my mother was anything but a mother after my parents' divorce, I couldn't tell Dad what had really happened when I lived in Kansas with her or near her. I blamed him for the change in her. But last year, I finally confessed how difficult those eight years in Kansas were. How I had turned into the parent and dealt with my mom's men and alcohol problems. I hated the divide that still existed between Mom and me. How our relationship felt superficial now.

"And for that I'm sorry." The guilt he still felt about it ran through his words.

"So why?" I came back to the original question.

He held the ball to him like a security blanket, but his eyes stayed fixed on me. He was owning it. "There isn't an easy answer. Selfishness, ego, alcohol, it's a bad combination and none of them a worthy excuse. You and your mother deserved better of me. The pain I caused both of you will live with me forever. The years I lost being in your life will always haunt me. I altered our family's future. Sometimes I wake up in the middle of the night and wish I could go back in time and undo that careless act. I would in a heartbeat if I could. But now all I can do is make sure I never repeat it."

"Do you still love Mom?"

He took a deep breath. When he exhaled, his breath filled the air in white wisps. "Your mother was my first love, the woman I planned to share my entire life with, and she gave me you. I wished we could have worked things out, but I'm not in love with her anymore. I love Felicity."

"I know you do. And I'm happy for you."

"You're my favorite kid. Speaking of which, how's your favorite kid?" Dad was done talking about the past.

My Josh grin erupted. It always came out when I talked about him. "He called me Mom last night."

"And you lived to tell the tale." Dad knew what Victoria was capable of.

"I could take her."

Dad laughed. "You know she's jealous of you."

"There's no reason to be."

"Sure there is. You and Ryan are happy; she's not. I think she thought leaving Ryan would solve all her problems, but now she has to face that she was the cause of most of them." He made a pretty three-point shot.

I found some energy and rebounded the ball. "I love you, Dad."

"I know, baby girl, and that means more to me than anything."

Dad kicked my butt before we headed back into pack. I came home with three boxes of pictures and photo albums. I wasn't sure what I would do with all of it. So many varying emotions were held in the boxes. For now, I set them in our home office closet. I would worry about them later. I had to finish my paper for my Counseling Process and Skills class that counted as my exam. I also had some more studying to do for the next day's exams. I could see the finish line, but there was what felt like walls to scale and fire pits to jump over to get there. It would be worth it, though. Now I needed to find some energy, and probably go buy a pregnancy test while I was alone.

I decided to head to Target first. I wasn't going to be able to concentrate until I knew one way or the other. The whole drive over I couldn't believe I was going to buy a pregnancy test. I was scared and excited on top of feeling nauseated. If I was pregnant, I hoped this feeling didn't last the entire time. I would be losing weight instead of gaining it at this rate.

I walked into Target covertly in my black athletic pants with black hoodie to match. I made eye contact with no one and only slipped down the female aisle when no one was looking. I passed by the tampons and pads, wondering if I would need any soon. I skirted the pregnancy prevention rows. Maybe I should have visited that section more often. I had never paid attention before to the fifty shelves of pregnancy tests. What the heck? Why were there so many choices? Which one was the right one? I tried to think back to the one Krissy used when she found out she was pregnant. It was a stick, and I remember two lines. But they had ones that were square and gave you a plus symbol and one that said pregnant or not pregnant. They were as cheap as a few dollars or as expensive as twenty.

Some random woman joined me in the aisle and gave me that look of "Get ready, sister." Was I ready? I loved being a stepmom— or goddess. But I didn't have to birth Josh, and I'd seen the videos with Krissy of the exorcist event they call birth. The babies even look alien when they come out. I remembered one where they talked about a fourth-degree perineal tear and repairs. And I remembered Krissy talking about bleeding nipples, stretch marks, and being up all night, not to mention how her lady parts felt like they were on fire for a few weeks after birth. What were we thinking, having sex? Birth control is only ninety-nine percent effective. I calmed myself with thoughts of Josh and how much I loved to cuddle Taylar Ann and took a deep breath. I thought about the times Ryan and I had talked about having our own and how I ached for it, and he did too. It would be worth it all, right?

I wasn't screwing around; I grabbed the most expensive digital pregnancy test they had. I went through self-checkout and wrapped that baby in two bags. No one was going to know about this until I said so. I'd drunk some water before I left, so I would be good to go when I got home. Come to think of it, I had been peeing more lately. Hmm.

I ran into the bathroom and locked the door. Sometimes Ryan came home early or for lunch to surprise me, which was only a cover for doing what had me peeing on a stick.

I read the instructions for the test. Why did they make it sound so freaking complicated? Something about catching your urine mid-stream. How did you even gauge that?

I was so nervous I peed on my hand and dropped the stupid stick in the toilet. Ugh! Good thing I got the box that had two tests in it. But I hated fishing things out of the toilet. I lived with a boy, so it wasn't an uncommon occurrence.

After I sanitized my hands and drank some more water, I turned on my laptop and waited to make sure I had a steady stream of urine ready to go. Men had no idea what an ordeal this was. I had no idea. I sat with my laptop on the edge of our bed tapping my fingers on the keys and staring blankly at the screen and title of my paper: "Why I Want to Become a Licensed Professional Counselor." When I first received the assignment, I thought it was a joke. It sounded like something I would have been assigned in junior high. But Dr. Rodan was serious. She was a tad eccentric, but I liked her Counseling Process and Skills class. And this paper gave me a lot to think about. It was the most personal I had ever been when writing a paper.

I always knew I wanted to help people, but after my parents' divorce, I wanted to make my world right again, to understand all the whys. I wanted to make sense of it all. More than anything, I've learned that some things never make sense, but it's our actions and attitudes that matter most. And our willingness to ask for help when we need it. I spent eight years hating the man who, before Ryan, I loved more than anyone. I was unwilling to forgive him because all I could see was what his actions had done to me and to my mom. I'd never stopped to think how they affected him. I'd never known anyone as remorseful as him. He lost his world too, and worse, he had to live knowing it was his fault. I would never agree with what he did, but this I knew: hate never solved a thing, and there are always two sides to a story, if we are willing to look past ourselves. Really, that was a lot of what marriage or couple counseling was— trying to help the couple see the best in each other and work on their own weaknesses instead of focusing on their partner's. We humans have a tough time with that.

You know what I was having a tough time with? Waiting. Did I have to pee? Or was I thinking I had to because I wanted to? I tried focusing on my paper, but all I could think about was that there could possibly be a life growing inside of me that Ryan and I had created. After reading the same sentence a hundred times, I said to heck with it. If worse came to worse, I would go buy a dozen more pregnancy tests until I knew for sure.

I took a deep breath, made sure I had a tight grip on that stick, and went with the flow, literally. This time I succeeded in urinating on the stick instead of my hand, though I still scrubbed my hands with a vengeance while I stared at the stick and waited for the words to appear like a magic eight ball. It said it could take up to two minutes, but I was an over achiever. I didn't even get soap on my hands before I had one of those life-changing moments.

Pregnant.

Seven

THE FAUCET CONTINUED TO RUN while I stared at the words on the stick. I was pregnant. I could rule out fatal disease now, but how could a tiny pea wreak so much havoc already?

My first instinct was to call Ryan. I had a hard time keeping anything from him. I'd ruined every surprise I'd ever planned for him because I was too excited to keep it from him. This time it was going to be different. I was going to think up something super cute and tell him on Christmas. It was only eleven days away. I could do it. Maybe?

Now to calculate my due date. The article online said to add seven days to the start date of your last period and then subtract three months. I calculated in my head. Mid-August. I was going to be huge preggers during the summer. Josh would be starting kindergarten that month. And I would be a few months into my internship. This could get interesting. At least it wasn't during tax season. Good job, baby, on that. Your accountant daddy and I thank you.

I rubbed my as-yet flat tummy. "Hey, little baby. I

hope you know what you're in for, choosing me to be your mommy."

Oh my gosh. I was going to be someone's mommy. Tears streamed down my face. I was going to be a mommy.

I securely wrapped up the pee stick and hid it in my nightstand until I thought up the cutest way ever to reveal to my husband that his sperm count was still alive and well. His little swimmers were apparently Olympic level, getting through the protective layers we had put in place. I knew Ryan would be so proud. I took a moment to stare at the framed wedding photo that sat on my nightstand. It was my favorite one of the three of us jumping on the trampoline after the informal ceremony. We were all mid-air. Joy jumped off the picture. Ryan and Josh looked so handsome in their tan cargo shorts and white button-up shirts. Best day of my life so far. Today was going to rank right up there.

Pregnant. I couldn't quit thinking about it. Waves of nausea and the constant feeling like I needed a nap wouldn't let me even if had wanted to, which I didn't.

I disposed of any evidence of what had gone down in the bathroom before I went back to work on my paper. I grabbed my notes and laptop and took them to bed with me. I figured I deserved to write my paper in bed, propped up by a mass of pillows. Ryan loved his pillows almost as much as me, which made convincing him to sleep under the Christmas tree a feat I was proud of.

I stared at the word-filled screen, thinking about my baby. Oh, I loved the sound of that. My baby. And what was my other baby going to think? He was going to be such a good big brother.

I had some distractions. First up was a text from Krissy. It was going to be so hard not to blab to her, but husband first, then best friend.

Our costumes for Saturday came in. They are so cute.

For the love, we were just passing out gifts at the senior living center. *Why do we need costumes, again? Can't we just wear Santa hats or something?*

It's a tradition to dress up like Mrs. Claus. And even Maviny thinks they're cuter than the picture I showed you. Maviny, her sister, was coming with us.

Fine. Do you want me to come pick mine up?

No. Just meet me at my place before, and we can all change together and drive over in the same car. Maviny wants to talk to you about Jay anyway.

Fun side note. Maviny and my ex-boyfriend, Jay, hooked up over Facebook in May. A friend of a friend sort of thing. I had liked one of Jay's posts, and Maviny had seen it and commented on it. That comment turned into several. The comments led to private messages. Messages led to phone calls. Phone calls to meeting in person. That first meeting was at our wedding. Maviny had no idea, she thought she was bringing Jay to a barbecue. When he showed up with Maviny, Ryan and I were surprised, but the show was going on. I think it was awkward for Jay, but he admitted it was closure. Nothing says closure like watching your ex-girlfriend get married.

It must not have been too awkward, because Maviny and Jay had been dating ever since, even though he still lived in Kansas and Maviny lived in Boulder, where she was finishing up school at CU and working part-time as a photographer. Dad had hired Maviny to do the wedding pictures. She was super talented. And it worked out great, since her parents, known as my dad's neighbors, the Lawtons, and Krissy and her husband Chance, a.k.a. the Wallaces, as they referred to themselves, were invited. They each booked a suite at the same resort where we would all be. If only we could get there. I needed a vacation.

What's up with Maviny and Jay? It was weird to ask about my ex-boyfriend's love life, but I was happy for him. Maviny loved him the way he deserved, not like I did— as a friend. Ryan wasn't all that thrilled that Jay was still present, but he knew my feelings for my ex were purely platonic, and hey, Ryan came with an ex-wife that would always be present.

She gave him an ultimatum. Fish or cut bait.

What? Why? It so sounded like Maviny, but no man wanted to hear that. And they had only been dating for six months.

She's been offered an internship with a studio in Ireland. She would leave in January and come back in June or July. When she told Jay, she said he acted indifferent.

Really? That didn't sound like him at all.

She's pretty upset. She doesn't think he feels the same way about her as she does about him.

This was like déjà vu for me. Ryan and I went through the same thing last year during Christmas when I thought for sure Ryan didn't want me. Worst Christmas ever. Which is why I was going to make this the best one ever. And now I had the best gift to give to him, a peed-on stick. Nothing says love like urine.

Poor Maviny. And what was wrong with Jay? Last time I saw them together over Thanksgiving, he looked happier than I had ever seen him. They were super-glued together the whole weekend. He even followed her to the bathroom once. We all laughed at him.

Maybe he's really stressed with work. He was an operations research analyst, and year end was a busy time for him.

Maybe.

Tell her I'm sure it will all work out and she can call me later if she needs to. Hopefully a lot later. I needed to focus, and I was doing a terrible job of it.

Study hard. See you Saturday.

Kiss your baby for me. I couldn't wait to kiss my own. But now I needed to focus.

I edited a few pages before my phone rang. It was a favorite number of mine, so I answered it.

"Hi, Mom." Ryan's mom, Kaye, asked if I would call her Mom and Guy, my father-in-law, Dad. It wasn't as awkward as I thought it would be. It almost sounded natural now.

"Hello, sweetie, how are you?" Her voice sounded unusually strained.

"I'm good. Just studying. How are you and Dad?"

She cleared her throat. "Terrific." Why did that sound so fake?

"Are you sure?"

"Of course, dear. I actually have some exciting news."

"Really?"

"Yes. I'm coming for Christmas."

What? "Oh. I thought you and Dad were going to Canada."

"You know, work calls."

I swore my father-in-law was a CIA agent but used working for the Department of Defense as a cover. He was always leaving for unexpected trips at unusual times. "Well, you know you are always welcome, but we're going to be in Beaver Creek for my dad's wedding."

"I know, dear. We were invited, but we had already booked our trip to Canada by the time we got the announcement. I'll just stay with you. You guys said you booked a suite, right?"

What did I say? We had a two-room suite, and the room we were putting Josh in had two double beds; but we were kind of hoping since there would be so much wedding chaos around that our suite would be like our own little sanctuary.

"We did," I stuttered.

"You don't mind, do you? I mean, I hate to be alone over the holidays, and Evan is doing who knows what with who knows who." Evan was Ryan's younger pig of a brother. He was up to four baby mamas now and probably working on number five. He paid more child support than most people made in a month. Each one of those moms and kiddos deserved every dime.

How could I say no? "When do you get here?"

"Monday. I'd come earlier, but I'm in charge of the Daughters of the Revolution Christmas Tea this weekend."

"That sounds nice."

"It will be fabulous. Can't wait to see you. Give my love to my boys. Love you, sweetie."

Yeah. Love you too. Why did I have a bad feeling about my holidays not being the magical event I had planned out in my mind? And it's not that I didn't love Kaye, but having her around was going to make seducing her son a lot harder. Her bedtime was a lot later than Josh's. And something seemed off about her sudden trip. But I didn't have time to worry about it.

Focusing on my paper was getting harder and harder. I had too many things to think about. Baby, Maviny and Jay, a wedding, Dad moving, Christmas shopping, my mother-in-law coming, a baby. Did I mention that I felt like crap?

Not sure when I fell asleep, but it was now dark. I remembered reading and typing some things. I was hoping some of it made sense.

Ryan frantically called my name. I opened my eyes to see that the only light in the room was from the glow of my laptop screen. I was surrounded by papers. It looked like I'd drooled on a few. Nice. How long had I been out? My body said not long enough. It was begging for more sleep.

But first I needed to calm my poor husband. "I'm in the bedroom," I called out. My voice wasn't working all that well.

Ryan rushed through the bedroom door and landed by my side, making the bed bounce. "Charlee, thank goodness you're okay. I texted you a few hours ago to tell you I was going to be late. When I noticed you never responded, I tried calling you. And I've been trying for the last hour."

I sat up as best I could. "I didn't mean to worry you. I guess I fell asleep."

He removed a post-it note from my hair before he picked up my nearby phone to check the volume and found it to be up. "Do I need to take you to urgent care?"

No, he didn't, but I supposed I should be making an appointment with an OB/GYN soon. One more thing to do. I reached up and rested my hand on his warm cheek. "I'm fine. I promise."

He took my hand from his cheek and kissed my palm. "Are you sure?"

"Positive." I looked at the mess that surrounded me. "What time is it?"

"Seven."

"I'm so behind. I need to finish editing my paper and study for my exam tomorrow." I was in panic mode. I reached for my laptop only to have my husband take it away from me.

"I'm going to edit your paper after I bring you dinner in bed, and then you're going back to sleep."

"I can't," I cried.

He refused to give me my laptop or take no for an answer. "Sleep will do you more good. And it's okay if you get a B." He knew what a freak I was about getting straight A's.

I gave him a pouty but I-love-your-guts smile. "You win."

He pecked my lips. "I love it when you say that."

"Thank you."

"It's my pleasure." He wasn't playing fair. He gathered

up all my papers, along with my laptop, and started walking out of the room. At least with all the craziness in my life I could always depend on him to do what he could to make it better. I hoped I did the same for him. But if I did get a B on my exam tomorrow, he'd better be ready for some tears.

Before Ryan got to the door I remembered the conversation I'd had with his mom. "P.S., your mom is coming for Christmas."

Ryan fumbled the papers and laptop, almost dropping it. Some papers did land on the floor. "What?"

My sentiments exactly.

Eight

ON FRIDAY, OUR ALARM WENT off at 4:30 a.m. It was an ungodly sound, but it meant in a half an hour our favorite kid was arriving and our holidays could begin. Sort of. I had one more exam to go. I was doing my best to pretend all was well. If not, Ryan would be hauling me to the doctor, and my surprise would be ruined. I'd been trying to stave off the nausea by grazing carb-filled snacks throughout the day. Pretzels and flat ginger ale were helping the most. And I was popping Josh's gummy vitamins on the sly, since I couldn't risk keeping any prenatal vitamins in the house yet.

Ryan rolled over after turning off the alarm. His warm hand found its way under my shirt and rested on my abdomen. "Good morning, gorgeous. How are you feeling?"

Wait. Did he know? Why was his hand on my stomach? Or was I being paranoid? But he never asked me how I was feeling. He normally kissed me awake. But he knew I hadn't been feeling well. Wednesday, I had broken down crying over the phone because I was sure I had failed my psychopathology exam. So maybe he was asking about my mental state.

I snuggled into my husband. "Perfect."

That was a major exaggeration. I could barely keep my eyes open, and as soon as he got up and hit the bathroom, I would be reaching into my nightstand drawer for the pretzels I had stashed there. But I was determined to keep this pregnancy a secret for eight more days. And Ryan was worried enough about the whole Victoria and Maxime thing. I didn't need him to worry about me unnecessarily. I knew what I had would eventually pass. I'd read online that by week twelve or fourteen I should be feeling better. It sounded like a long time away. August sounded like forever. I wanted to get my hands on this baby wreaking havoc in my body.

Ryan wrapped his arms around me. "That's what I like to hear."

The relief in his voice made the half untruth worth it.

His hands drove down all my curves. "I found the perfect Christmas gift for you yesterday."

"It won't be as good as what I got you."

"We should bet on this."

"Nothing says the spirit of Christmas like turning gift-giving into a sport."

He laughed in my ear. "I suppose you're right, but it's going to take a lot to top my gift."

"I'm not worried." I pushed him away in a playful manner. His morning breath was getting to me. This baby was making his or her presence known. "We'd better get up."

Even in the dim light I could see the question in his eyes. "If I didn't know better I would think you were trying to kick me out of bed."

He wasn't making this secret-keeping stuff easy on me. I tried not to breathe in too deep when I pecked his lips, hoping he didn't take that as an invitation to do some exploration of my mouth, at least not until he swished some mouthwash or brushed those pearly whites of his. His breath had never bothered me before, so this was new territory for us. "I love you, and there is nothing better than being in bed with you, but I would rather not have to explain to Josh or Victoria why it took us so long to answer the door." That was all true.

He crushed his lips against mine. I held my breath the entire time. This baby-growing stuff was serious. How could I have any aversion to Ryan? But he only had himself to blame. It was one of his guys that broke through Fort Knox. At least, I assumed it was only the one. I didn't have my first doctor appointment until January. I had called yesterday to make that appointment and made the office swear to only talk to me directly if they had to contact me before Christmas. I was even up for giving them code names, but the lady at the appointment desk assured me that wouldn't be necessary. Too bad, that could have been fun.

"You drive a hard bargain, Mrs. Jensen-Carter. I guess Josh is young for the sex talk." He turned to get out of bed. It wasn't a moment too soon. I needed to take a breath. But he turned right back toward me. "By the way, when we have kids, what do you want their last name to be, Carter or Jensen-Carter?"

His question made me forget about his breath. Why was he asking this now? He couldn't know, could he? He would just come out and ask. Right? "I haven't thought about it." I tried to act unaffected. "What are your thoughts?" I figured it was something we should discuss.

He shrugged his shoulders. "Honestly, I'm fine either way."

"Really?"

"I think your dad would like it if his name got passed on."

That was the reason I hyphenated. "I think he would like that, too, but we have a while to decide."

"I can't wait." Longing filled his voice.

"Me either. Now, get ready."

He saluted me. "Yes, ma'am."

Dang, that was sexy, but not enough to overcome his breath. Eight more days, I told myself, then I could tell Ryan to bring breath mints to bed with us.

All I did to prepare for the early morning arrival was to eat some pretzels, get rid of the evidence I had eaten any, and throw my hair in a ponytail. My T-shirt and flannel pajama bottoms would have to do. I'm sure Victoria would be dressed like she was hitting the town instead of the airport.

My prediction was accurate. Ryan opened the door to find a sleepy Josh and Victoria wearing some faux fur jacket paired with a jumper and some serious high heels. But her eyes were red, and it looked like she had cried off her makeup. This had never happened before in my presence. Her hold on Josh was different too. She was always reluctant to let him go whenever she dropped him off or we picked him up, but this was… heartbreaking. I could see her heart break.

Ryan and I shared a concerned glance before moving out of the way to let Victoria and Josh in. Normally I would have pulled Josh into my arms for a hug, but I was afraid of what that would have done to Victoria. Her fragile emotions were screaming out of her eyes.

Ryan took Josh's backpack from Victoria. Josh had his own set of clothes and toys here, but there were a few of his favorite things that he shuttled back and forth between houses. As soon as Ryan relieved Victoria of the backpack she fell to her knees and wrapped Josh up tighter than she was wound up.

"I love you, and you can call me anytime." She bathed Josh with her tears.

Josh was so sleepy he was barely coherent, but he hugged his mommy and murmured something like I love you.

Victoria's iron grip continued. "Have a Merry Christmas, honey."

"I can't wait for Santa." Josh wasn't helping his mother's mental state, but I don't think he truly understood how long Victoria would be gone. All he knew in his young life was being shared between parents. To him this was a normal drop-off. To Victoria this was the end of the world, from the looks of it.

Not sure if it was the early hour or pregnancy brain— which was a real thing, by the way— but something came out of my mouth I thought I would never say.

"You don't have to go." I felt like Victoria needed the permission to say no, even if that meant a huge part of my Christmas dreams would be dashed to pieces. We would still get Josh for Christmas, even if she stayed, since we gave her Thanksgiving in exchange. But we would only get him for a week.

Victoria lifted her head off Josh's shoulder, and instead of the ire I thought I would see, there was a flicker of gratitude. But it was short-lived.

She squinted her eyes. "Why would I do that?"

She stood up but kept her arm around Josh, who looked ready to fall back asleep in his old-man pajamas. Victoria was ever proper, even with Josh's sleeping attire.

I reminded myself to be kind. I couldn't imagine leaving Josh for two weeks, especially over the holidays. "Because maybe you're not sure this is what you want."

Her jaw dropped, but she recovered quickly and snapped it shut. "Of course I'm sure." Not even she believed it. She put another death grip on Josh while addressing Ryan. "Make sure if any of your plans change, I know about them. Do your best not to let him eat too much junk. And don't forget sunscreen if you let him ski, which I'm not all that thrilled about."

"I wanna ski." Josh perked up some.

"Want to," his mother corrected him. Victoria was a private tutor and a stickler when it came to grammar. One time she corrected a text I sent to her. She told me I shouldn't end my sentences with a preposition. I responded back with a link informing her it was perfectly acceptable nowadays. I sent a winky face with it, so I figured that was okay. She, on the other hand, was furious. I got a research paper back on why it was a crime against humanity. I was impressed she could write such a long text, considering she was old-school and hadn't learned how to use her thumbs when she texted— she did the old index-finger routine. It was painful to watch.

Ryan took Josh's hand, even though Victoria wasn't letting go. "He'll be fine. We signed him up for ski school, and I've already packed the sunscreen and a helmet for him."

Victoria ignored Ryan and knelt one more time to love on Josh. She filled his cheeks with kisses while tears ran down her own. Josh was the sweetest kid ever and wiped her cheeks. "Don't cry, Mommy. I'll wear sunscreen."

She laughed, albeit a little. I didn't know she could do that. "I'll call you every day," she choked out.

He nodded his cute head and hugged his mommy one more time before making his way to me. "Bye, Mommy." He waved.

Victoria stood still, looking unsure about what she should do; but with a shake of her head, her steel resolve was back. She squared her shoulders and marched out our door into the bitter-cold December morning. As soon as she was out of sight, I gave Josh a big hug.

"Ready for some cartoons and hot chocolate?"

"Yes!" He raced me to the couch and won, hands down. My body was in no mood for racing, even a tiny one. While Josh and I snuggled under a blanket, Ryan made Josh hot chocolate. I declined one of my favorite drinks. If this baby hated chocolate, we were in trouble. I wasn't sure I could do months without it.

"Mom, can we have pancakes for breakfast?"

I melted on the couch. He was getting a "yes" anytime he called me Mom, even if it meant cooking while feeling like I wanted to puke. "Sure, big guy, but let's wait until the sun is up."

Josh drank his hot chocolate, and within fifteen minutes he was asleep, snuggled against me while I rested against a worried Ryan.

"I don't feel good about you know who," Ryan whispered to not wake up Josh. "You saw her reaction this morning."

"I did, but she's a grown woman. And he hasn't done anything."

"That's the point. He doesn't even try to be involved in Josh's life, and what kind of man makes a woman choose between him or her son?"

"I don't think he's forcing her to go."

"I know. I just can't stand the thought of him being Josh's stepfather."

"Victoria can't stand me."

"Don't take it personally; she didn't like me most of our marriage."

That made me incredibly sad. "Her loss is my gain."

He kissed the side of my head. "Sorry I'm so rattled by this."

"I get it." I was also beginning to see my plan of no interference from the ex-wife during my holidays was going up in smoke. She would be present even when she wasn't.

Nine

Josh went in to work with Ryan, since I had one more final and some shopping to do. Ryan was hoping to groom Josh to take over the firm one day. My dad was all for it. As long as it wasn't me, I was good; I'd rather poke my eyes out. The day I walked away from being a CPA at Jensen-Carter Accounting was one of the best days of my life.

Today was really my last opportunity to get Ryan's gift before all the wedding and Christmas chaos kicked into full gear. I'd been scouring the internet trying to find a clever or cute way to announce our bundle of joy. Nothing fit. Ryan wasn't a cutesy kind of person, and neither was I. The only thing I could think of was matching running shoes, a pair for him and one for the baby. That would be well over a hundred dollars, but this was more than a Christmas gift. I tried to justify breaking the rules. And let's be honest, Ryan expected me to. Matching running shoes it was.

I also had to buy a shower gift for Felicity. What do you get a couple that has everything? And I had just helped my dad throw away a bunch of things he didn't want to move into their new place.

I sighed when I drove by my dad's house on the way out of our neighborhood. He and Felicity were closing on their townhome today. He didn't close on his house until mid-January, but today was the end of an era. It was a game changer. I hoped it meant that this marriage was going down. Owning property together was a big commitment. I felt so grown up when Ryan added me to the deed of our house. Who would have ever thought I would own 1937 Mulberry Lane, home of my teenage crush? I knew the day the Carter family moved in next door was life changing. All I had to do was grow up. I still thanked my in-laws for moving next door to us all those years ago and then selling their house to Ryan after his divorce, when they moved to D.C.

I headed to campus first to take my final in counseling theories. It was my least favorite class this semester, which was unfortunate, because I enjoyed the coursework; but the professor was biased and a Sigmund Freud lover. Not like Freud didn't have value, but the world of psychology had so much more to offer nowadays. And if I had to analyze one more of my dreams, it could get ugly.

I'd spoken to soon— my exam was to analyze last night's dream.

How could that be my final? Did he know how much I'd studied? Maybe I should be grateful, but I was a little creeped out that the guy wanted to know so much about our dreams. What was he doing with that information? And how do you really grade dream analysis? What if I hadn't dreamt anything? That wasn't the case, but some people had a hard time remembering their dreams.

Not me. I vividly remembered that I was late for school and kept trying to get ready, but all these strange people were in our house, and our house didn't look like our house. And every time I got up to get ready or take a shower, someone would stop me or would be using the five bathrooms in this make-believe home. In real life, I would never have five bathrooms. Three was way too many to clean, and did I mention we had a little boy at our place? That got me to thinking. What if we had another little guy? I would be cleaning urine all the time. Anyway, back to my dream. I finally got frustrated and yelled for everyone to get out; that's when I woke up. I hated dreams like that. There was a realism that was frustrating.

I wasn't sure how much stock I put into dream analysis, but I could take a guess why I dreamt I was late. I was late for something, but that was none of my professor's business. And this pregnancy had me not feeling like myself, so that could be the reason our home didn't look like our home. And all the extra people could represent my mother-in-law coming unexpectedly and how I felt like even though Victoria wasn't present, she was. But really this was no one's business, so I used a dream from a few weeks ago where I got a recording contract singing silly preschool songs like "Ring Around the Rosie," a popular tune with Josh. And I told them I could only sing if I was bouncing on a trampoline, so the record executives brought one into the studio. It could totally happen. Let's just hope it could get me an A on my final.

With the weirdest test ever over, I headed to a running shoe store near campus in Fort Collins. I couldn't risk going to Ryan's favorite shoe store near us in Loveland. We were too well known there. Ryan spent more money on shoes than I did. A fact I loved to tease him about. I only hoped this place carried Ryan's favorite brand. It wasn't a run-of-the-mill brand. Ryan was a running shoe connoisseur.

I snacked on pretzels while I browsed. It was probably against some rule, but I didn't care. They were the only thing keeping me functioning. I was already thinking about how to sneak up several bags on our trip.

It's not like I'd ever been a huge fan of the salty snacks, but I praised their existence now. And before too long Ryan was going to get suspicious when all the caps to the ginger ale kept disappearing. If only they sold that stuff without carbonation. He already thought it was weird I had a sudden craving for the golden liquid. Someday soon he would know it was all his fault.

I was in luck, and the store carried the shoe I was looking for. Unfortunately, that brand didn't make baby shoes, so I had to buy our baby a different brand that was close to the same gray as Ryan's. I loved saying "our baby," or thinking it. And oh my gosh, if baby shoes weren't the cutest things ever. It made me want to go out and buy some baby outfits. I restrained myself. I knew if I did the surprise would be over. I would be showing Ryan those baby clothes and shoes before I could help myself. Besides, I still had to buy a shower gift.

Shopping for these types of things wasn't my strong

suit. It made me all the more glad Ryan and I didn't torture our friends and family with showers and all the typical pre-wedding nonsense. I think Dad felt the same way, but Felicity's mother would never hear of it. She was adamant that Felicity get exactly what she deserved, even if it wasn't what Felicity wanted at all. Dad played along because I think part of him felt guilty about the no-children thing, and he knew how hard it had been for Felicity to watch him get over my mother. She stood by him when I think most women in her position would have left, thinking it was a lost cause. For that reason alone, I would always love Felicity. With all that, I wanted to get Felicity something that said she belonged to our family.

My brain wasn't working all that well after finals and all the nutrition I'd been denying it. I had lost two pounds already. And I was too tired to go from store to store in search of the perfect gift. I bet Felicity was tired too. I remembered Krissy being a wreck right before her wedding. So maybe Felicity could use some TLC, and maybe we could do it together. I stopped by the spa where we'd held Krissy's bachelorette party last year and got a spa package for Felicity and myself. It would be something we could do together once she and Dad got back from their honeymoon. With it, I would write a note to convey how happy I was she was joining our family.

Krissy called as I rushed home in hopes of beating Ryan so I could wrap his gift up with the pregnancy test. Taylar Ann was babbling in the background. She jabbered about everything. Not sure what she was saying, but it was freaking adorable, and I couldn't wait to have one.

"Hey, Kris. What's up?"

"Do you still have the shoes you wore to my wedding?"

"Why?" I'd buried those uncomfortable babies in a box when I moved next door to shack up with my husband. The only reason I kept them was because I was wearing them the first time Ryan and I danced together. One of the best nights ever. It was the first time he admitted I was more than just grown up. He called me beautiful and annoyingly charming. I was still good with those adjectives.

"Could you bring them tomorrow to my house?"

"What for?"

"Just trust me."

"Oh, no, no. Last time I did that, I ended up in those hooker heels, half naked at your wedding."

"And you're welcome. Ryan couldn't take his eyes off you."

"You still didn't answer my question, why do you want me to bring them?"

She paused and then paused some more. "I need them for... a comparison?"

"You used to be a better liar. What's up?"

"It's just... they may go better with your costume than the boots that came with it."

"I thought we were wearing Mrs. Claus outfits."

"We are."

"Mrs. Claus never walked Colfax." Colfax was a famed street in Denver known for those who belonged to the oldest profession.

"She also never looked as good as you are going to look in her dress, so bring the dang shoes. I love you. Bye." She hung up.

Why did I have a bad feeling about this?

Ten

CHRISTMAS BREAK HAD OFFICIALLY STARTED. Two weeks of no work, no school, no exes, and no trouble. Fingers crossed. Ryan's mom was putting a little blip in our plans, but I loved her, and she was drama free, so it wasn't a big deal. And I didn't want her to be alone for Christmas. I felt bad that Ryan's dad would be traveling for business— a.k.a. spying— over the holidays.

Saturday chore music was alive and well in the Jensen-Carter home. During the month of December, we swapped classic rock for Christmas carols. We jammed out to "Rockin' Around the Christmas Tree" and "Jingle Bell Hop" while we swept and dusted between our silly dances. I pretended to be energetic. Ryan bought it hook, line, and sinker. He was so worried about the Victoria situation that he was happy to pretend his wife was well even if she'd fallen asleep at 8:00 the night before. I must be growing a giant who needed every resource available. And I was so grateful Josh requested waffles for breakfast instead of eggs or bacon. Cracking an egg or smelling bacon would have been the death of me.

Volunteering at the nursing home gave me a great excuse for not eating much— I was in a hurry to get over to Krissy's. And even though I had an uneasy feeling about the hooker heels, I trudged down to our basement to find them. I took a moment to reminisce while I searched through the box I was sure they were in. I found the ticket stubs to the One Republic concert Ryan took me to on our first date. They were a little tattered. I had thrown them away at one point when Ryan had one of his episodes, as I now referred to them. But I'd had a change of heart and fished them out of the trash. I'm so glad I did. It was the night of my last first date and kiss. The night my life changed. I ran my hand across my abdomen. We were in store for another huge change.

Buried beneath more of my mementos were those dang, strappy high heels. Why was I unearthing these? If Krissy thought I was wearing them again, she was crazy. I didn't care what the boots looked like that came with the costume; they had to be better than the hooker heels. I was only bringing them so Krissy wouldn't whine.

Ryan grinned at the shoes when I emerged from the basement door in our kitchen. "One of my favorite memories is of you wearing those in your cutoffs. I wouldn't remind a repeat."

I remembered that day too. I had been so embarrassed Ryan caught me while I practiced walking in them for Krissy's wedding. "If memory serves me correctly, you laughed at me."

He pulled me to him, and, thankfully, his breath was clean and smelled normal, like honey. "I only laughed to keep away thoughts of wanting to ravish my partner's daughter."

"Uh-huh."

He brushed my lips. "You have no idea how hard it was to resist you."

"You seemed to manage." I loved teasing him.

He groaned against my mouth. "You've obliterated all my defenses."

"Is that so?" I let the heels drop so I could use my hands for better things. And I was just about to until—

"MOM!"

Being a newlywed with a child was tricky business. Ryan sighed but smiled. "I'll take a rain check." He had plenty to cash in.

I pecked his lips and rushed off to see what Josh needed. I found Josh in his room shooting hoops with his miniature basketball and the hoop we'd installed on his wall. It was a good alternative on cold winter days. "What's up, big guy?"

"I want you to see how far away I can make a basket."

By the sound of his call I'd thought he might need me to fish his toothbrush out of the toilet again. You don't know how happy I was that wasn't it. "Show me what you got."

In a stellar move I'd taught him, he ran back to the far side of his room, turned, and shot in a seamless action. His form was spot-on, and he followed through. Too bad the ball dropped a few feet in front of the basket.

Disappointment filled his eyes. "Aww, man!"

"That's okay. Try again. This time drop your elbow more, and aim higher."

It took him a few tries, but he got there. "Yes!" He high-fived me. "I can't wait to start basketball."

We had signed him up through the recreation center to play on a youth basketball league that started in January. I planned on turning all our kids into basketball players. Ryan would teach them how to be track and field stars. My insides smiled amid the pukey feeling, thinking about all the things we had to look forward to.

"Me, either. We can play some more when I get home. Now you need to get ready. Your daddy's going to take you to see Santa and to lunch while I go help Aunt Krissy."

She wasn't really his aunt, but the closest thing we had on our side since I was an only child and Ryan only had a brother. And Krissy was like a sister to me.

"Yes! I can't wait to tell Santa what I want."

"What are you going to ask for?"

So far he had been refusing to say, which was unlike him. Ryan and I were hoping it was the laser tag set we'd purchased him specifically for Santa to bring. He'd seemed excited about it when we took him down the toy aisle at Target a few weeks ago. And he'd loved the times we had taken him to play laser tag. We weren't sure why he was being so secretive, but not even Victoria could get it out of him. Santa would come to her house after she got back. Speaking of her, she was safe and sound in Madrid. She'd sounded abnormally cheerful when talking to Ryan early this morning. I didn't know she could be cheerful, even if she was faking it. Ryan didn't say anything, but I saw the worry in his eyes.

Josh had a smile that mirrored his dad's when he was

trying to be sneaky. Ryan's idea of being sneaky was not telling me where he was taking me to dinner. I had a feeling Josh was going to be more devious than his dad.

"It's a secret." Josh wasn't giving up a thing.

I was going to have to tell Ryan to get as close as he could to Santa and Josh. Too bad I wasn't taking Josh. Ryan wasn't good at being covert or willing to embarrass himself to get the job done. I would have ditched Krissy and Maviny, but I didn't want to let the senior living center down. Maybe Ryan could pay off an elf. I would mention it to him.

I said my goodbyes to my men and left with the hooker heels and a bag of pretzels stashed in my purse. I had snuck flat ginger ale into one of my water bottles. Seven more days of sneaking around.

Krissy and Chance had moved from Fort Collins back to Loveland this summer when Chance started working at the Walgreens Pharmacy a few miles from our house. They bought a cute fixer upper in an older part of town. Colorado housing prices were skyrocketing, so it was all they could afford. I wished they could have afforded my dad's house, but Krissy thought it would be weird to live next door to her parents. She teased me about doing it, but it had its perks. Dad was a great babysitter, and he made us dinner from time to time. Not to mention all the basketball we got in. I was going to get depressed if I kept thinking about it.

Dad seemed happy, though; he'd dropped by last night to show us the keys to the new place. In six days, he would be a married man.

Krissy's house made me smile when I pulled up. The brick rambler was decked out in pink Christmas lights. Even in the daylight the pink lights popped. How she talked Chance into them I had no clue. Okay, so maybe I did, but I wasn't mentioning it. Pink adorned the trees and lined the house's roof. It was something to behold at night. It so fit Krissy's perky and sparkly personality. And it matched the pink tree inside. Poor Chance never had a chance.

I grabbed the dang shoes and walked up the concrete walk. I didn't bother knocking. I could hear Krissy and Maviny talking inside, more like Krissy comforting Maviny. This wasn't good. I walked into disarray. Not only was Maviny a mess, but Krissy's kitchen was being renovated, and the remnants spilled over into the living room. There were new dark-stained cupboards sitting in the corner, and it looked like Taylar Ann had decided to redecorate the pink tree. White ornaments rolled around on the ground near the tree.

Krissy was bouncing a fussy Taylar Ann in her arms while Maviny cried on her shoulder. I wasn't sure which girl to take until Taylar Ann reached out her arms to me. Her blonde, wispy hair was finally coming in. What she lacked in hair she made up for with her big blue eyes. I dropped the shoes before taking her and cuddling her close. She quieted, allowing me to focus on the scene in front of me.

"What's going on?"

Maviny howled against her sister.

Krissy patted her back. "Jay decided to keep on fishing."

"What?" I had texted Jay a couple of days ago to see what was going on, but I got a generic text back of, *No need to worry.*

"Did he say why?" I dared to ask.

Maviny steeled herself and stood up tall, wiping her porcelain cheeks. She was a pretty girl with blonde hair and blue eyes like her sister and niece. All the Lawton women including their mom, Ann, had that cute, short, cheerleader look going for them. I always felt like an Amazonian woman next to them.

Maviny shuddered and took a cleansing breath. "He said it would be better for me to go with no strings attached, and maybe when I returned from Ireland we could pick up where we left off." She was doing her best not to get emotional again. "If that's what he wants, then I'm going to find the sexiest Irish man available and maybe never come back."

Every word sounded like an empty threat. That was the hurt talking.

"Did you tell him that what you really wanted was to stay?"

The waterworks started again. "No, because if he really loved me he would have asked me to stay." She fell against me even though I was holding the baby.

Krissy was quick to take Taylar Ann out of my arms.

I wrapped my arms around Maviny. There she snottily cried into my chest. I patted her back. "Maybe this is his way of telling you he loves you."

"What?" She continued her bawl-fest on my favorite blue sweater.

"He probably doesn't want you to miss out on this great opportunity, so he thinks he's being supportive. And you wouldn't be the first woman who left him for a job opportunity." No need to mention that I was the other woman. Everyone knew. "That could make him think twice."

Her crying instantly ceased. "You think so?"

"It sounds like something he would do." I hoped I wasn't giving her false hope where there was none, but Jay acted so smitten around her, it was hard to imagine him just up and changing his mind.

"Would you please talk to him?"

"Um... I think it would be best if you talked to him and laid out all the cards."

"Please, CJ," my childhood friends and parents still used my nickname sometimes, "you're like a therapist and you know all the right things to say. And Jay trusts you. And what if he doesn't really love me?" She clung to me.

"I'm not a therapist yet, and it might be awkward for Jay if I talk to him, considering we dated."

"It won't be." She sounded desperate. "I thought he was the one." She knew how to work the whole guilt thing.

"Okay."

"You're the best, CJ."

I was a sucker for my friends and love.

Jay was getting a phone call when this was all said and done. Miscommunication and unmet expectations killed relationships. I would say this was the case here. Maviny expected Jay to react the way she imagined he would, the way she would have if the roles had been reversed. Instead he acted logically. Which wasn't bad, but Maviny was an emotional creature. And she was scared of being rejected. Sure, she told him she loved him, but that was different than telling someone you were willing to change your life because of them. The stakes were higher in that scenario, making the chance for hurt greater. Jay was probably scared of being hurt too. But that was my semi-professional opinion. I would have to talk to Jay to know for sure. How did I get myself wrapped up in these things? I was going to send them a bill if this all worked out.

Chance arrived home from his pickup game at the rec center in time to take Taylar Ann so we could get ready. Taylar Ann's smile said Daddy was her favorite. She had the man wrapped around her finger. It was cute to watch Chance talk to his daughter. I couldn't wait to see how Ryan would be around our baby. I already knew he was a terrific dad, but Josh was three and a half before I entered the picture, so I'd missed the baby years.

Krissy dragged us back to her bedroom to change. Her room had clothing and half-empty suitcases strewn about. It looked like she was packing early for the trip to Beaver Creek. They were arriving a day after us, on the twenty-second. I noticed a pair of Krissy's ski pants draped on the rocking chair in her room. They reminded me I was going to need to come up with a good excuse for why I wasn't skiing. I read that you can put your pregnancy at risk if you ski and fall. I was a good skier, but I didn't want to take any risks. I was carrying priceless cargo.

I noticed some other articles of clothing lying on her bed. And the answer was nope, nope, and nope. Krissy's half angel, half devil eyes met mine before I could get out my displeasure. I was having flashbacks of being in the bathroom at Chili's where she made me try on the brides-maid dress for her wedding.

"Aren't they cute?" Krissy cut me off at the pass.

I eyed the Mrs. Claus outfits that must have come from an elf shop, or maybe the same place Krissy picked out her bridesmaids' dresses. There was no way I was wearing the tiny dress. I didn't even bring Spanx.

"You told me you gave them my measurements and that you ordered the right size."

"It's a size four." Krissy played innocent.

"A children's four, maybe. Did you tell them how tall I was?"

Krissy and Maviny shared a sly glance. "Well... they only come in one length."

"I'm going to get taller friends."

Maviny and Krissy laughed at me.

I folded my arms and glared at the beautiful *short* women. "I'm not wearing that."

Krissy hugged my stiff body. "Come on, CJ, it's for a good cause, and you're going to look amazing in it."

"You said that last time you talked me into wearing a barely-there dress."

"This dress it totally different. It has long sleeves and fur. And you totally have the body to pull it off, just like last time. At least try it on."

I scanned the red velvet dresses lined with faux fur. A black belt went around the middle. It would have been cute if it was several inches longer or if I was several inches shorter, like my friends.

Maviny picked up my dress, while Krissy unceremoniously started lifting my sweater off me.

"Hey, now. Only one person gets to undress me." I smacked Krissy's hands away.

"Ooo. I bet Ryan would love this dress." Krissy was undeterred, and before I knew it I was in my panties and bra. Yep, flashbacks of Chili's played in my mind. At least I wasn't standing on a germy bathroom floor covered in toilet paper.

Maviny held out the dress for me to step into. "We have to hurry, or we'll be late."

"Fine." I stepped into the Mrs. Claus-meets-Vixen dress. I shimmied into it, and Krissy zipped me up.

"Have you lost weight?" Krissy asked.

"Ryan and I are training for that half marathon." I played off the weight loss.

"Oh, yeah, I forgot about that." Krissy believed me, thank goodness. "How's that going?"

"I'm surviving. I haven't run this week, though, because of finals." And for another good reason. I turned around so I could look in Krissy's floor-length mirror. Before I could, Maviny and Krissy wagged their eyebrows. That couldn't be good.

The scheming sisters parted and gave me a clear shot of my long, bare legs with no hint of a tan left on them, topped with a child's dress. I looked like I belonged on the naughty list. "I can't wear this in public."

"It's not public. It's the senior center. Besides, you look hot." Krissy flashed me a you-know-you-want-to-do-this smile.

Maviny played with my hair, but her eyes were still watering up from time to time. "I like that you've let your hair grow out."

I hadn't on purpose. I had been too busy for a haircut. But I kind of liked the way my ash hair fell past my shoulders now. It looked nice when I had time to really style it. I threw it up in a messy bun most days. Today I'd put some beachy waves in it. But hair was the least of my concerns. I turned sideways and on my tip toes to see where the fur trim landed near my nether regions. It was too close for my comfort.

"Let's get you in some shoes. It makes the whole outfit." Krissy dove under her bed.

I thought that was weird until she pulled out the boots that came with the outfit. No wonder she was hiding them. They were much different than the cute little elf boots she'd showed me online when she chose the outfit. Now, here I was staring at lace black boots with a heel to rival the red hooker heels. I didn't even know you could make boots from lace. "What are these? Did you buy those at Tramps R Us?"

"Ha-ha, no. They didn't have the original shoes in your size, so they sent these."

"If you think I'm wearing those, you're out of your freaking mind." And why in the world would they go from cute little booties to booty call boots?

"I thought you would say that, so I asked you to bring the red shoes."

"Why didn't you just tell me to buy some new shoes?"

"I know how busy you've been and how much you hate shoe shopping. I was doing you a favor."

I put my hands on my face. "What are the odds of me leaving this house fully dressed?"

Krissy wrapped her arms around me. "I love you, CJ. Just think how much holiday cheer you're going to bring to the men in the nursing home. Because of you, they can die happy."

I rolled my eyes at her. "This is absolutely without a doubt the last time you are ever buying me clothes. And the red shoes are being retired after today. Got it?"

She nodded. "You have my word."

"Good. Now go get me the dang shoes."

Eleven

I THINK I MADE SOME new friends at the center. I might even make it into some final wills and testaments, according to the frisky senior citizens. One poor man with dementia thought I was a stripper and tried to shove a dollar bill down… well we won't mention it. Good thing I have good reflexes and he had poor aim.

Ryan was a huge fan of the outfit. I texted him a picture of it before we left for the nursing home to get his opinion. His response: *Please tell me you get to keep it.*

I admit, once I forgot I looked like Mrs. Claus' naughty twin, I enjoyed my time at the nursing home. It reminded me how blessed I was to have family and friends around. With each gift I delivered, I took the time to talk to those who could or wanted to. Even if they couldn't speak, I would take their hand, anything to let them know they weren't alone. One of the women especially touched my heart. She didn't say much, but she didn't want to let go of my hand. She stroked mine so tenderly while calling me a cutie pie. I detected a Southern accent. Her frail, translucent hand was soft to the touch. Each age spot told of how old she was. It was amazing how much human emotion could be conveyed through such a simple touch.

I'd looked around her tiny room only filled with the bare necessities and a few photos from years gone by. There was one of her wedding day. She was a beautiful bride in a simple silk gown. Her groom was dressed in a military uniform. I bet there was a story to tell there. The picture next to it was of her as a mother with two babies on the hip and a toddler on the floor playing by her feet. She looked exhausted, but content. Treasured memories, I'm sure. I would have liked to ask her about them, but she faded in and out of sleep, never loosening her grip of my hand. I stayed until she slept soundly. For a moment, I forgot about how ill I felt and how uncomfortable I was in that dress. I was reminded of the spirit of the season.

I left the nursing home wanting to be a better person. To raise even better people. It was almost the perfect way to start off my holidays. Proper attire was the only thing lacking.

I tried to keep the holly jolly attitude from the nursing home all weekend, especially when I entered the lair, I mean home, of Celia McLaughlin, Felicity's mother the following day. Candy and Eden, her sisters-in-law, were throwing the shower, but Celia was hosting at her home in Longmont, about a half hour away from Loveland if the traffic was decent. Celia was an interesting character to me; her home and lifestyle were simple. Her husband— Felicity's father— had died several years ago, leaving Celia to live off a meager life insurance policy and her job as a librarian for one of the high schools in Longmont. Yet she insisted that Felicity have a wedding fit for a queen. My dad was happy to oblige. But it left poor Felicity stuck in the middle. I know Felicity offered to pay for what she could, but my dad wouldn't hear of it. He figured it was *their* money anyway. I do wish, though, that Felicity felt like she could disagree with her mother, or at least stand up to her when she felt uncomfortable.

I understood the delicate balance of trying to maintain a good relationship with your mom when how you saw life and situations was vastly different than her. Take my mom for instance, who was upset with me because I was spending Christmas with my dad again. Ryan and I offered to go to Kansas to spend Thanksgiving with her and her husband, Mark, but they decided to spend Thanksgiving with one of Mark's daughters in Wisconsin. She couldn't understand why Dad had to get married on Christmas Eve. It wouldn't have been my first choice, but it wasn't my choice. Regardless, I wouldn't miss their wedding for the world. Just like I didn't miss Mom's and Mark's.

I kept wondering how happy my mom really was; she wasn't the woman I grew up with. I ached for a real relationship with her, especially now that I was pregnant. I felt like ever since she married Mark I was an afterthought. Thinking about it made that holly jolly attitude fade.

I took a deep breath and walked with care up the icy stone path to Celia's home. We had gotten a light dusting of snow overnight. The forecast said we were in for some more snow this week in the mountains. It would make for some great skiing, at least for Ryan and Josh. I was still trying to come up with some plausible excuse for why I was skipping out on one of my favorite activities, one that wouldn't worry or make my husband suspicious.

Ryan kind of had me suspicious. This morning he'd made another offhanded comment when we woke up with Josh in our bed, which wasn't an unusual occurrence. Sometimes Josh got scared at night, and I was a huge sucker for his dimples and cuddling, so I let him crawl right in between Ryan and me. It worked out well, too, since Josh's breath didn't bother me like Ryan's.

Anyway, Ryan had mentioned that we would need a bigger bed once we had a baby if I kept letting Josh sleep with us. Ryan knew me well enough to know that any babies we had would be coming to bed with us from time to time. But why was he suddenly talking about babies? I hid all the evidence that I was pregnant. And I was doing my best to act "normal."

It was time to act normal again. I knocked on the door with a cute sign that read, *Bride to be Inside.* The noise from inside was already spilling out. I was a little late to the party. I'd gotten caught up in an indoor basketball game with Josh and lost track of time. I used our time together to try to get the kid to spill the beans about what he asked Santa for. Ryan had felt awkward paying off an elf and apparently didn't want to seem like a creeper by getting too close. I could see his point, but I didn't want Josh to be disappointed Christmas morning. But my big guy's lips were locked up tight. He kept giving me his devious little smile. We were going to have to watch him.

I loved that he was a tad sneaky, though. It was good for the soul.

Things that were not good for the soul— Celia. She opened the door and gave me a squinty-eyed smile. "Well, it's nice of you to finally join us."

I walked in with my gift, not bothering to make an excuse for my tardiness. "It's so nice to see you." I managed to get that out without gritting my teeth.

She took the gift bag, no doubt to see if what I got my future stepmother was up to her expectations, before she placed it on the gift table. "You can hang your coat up there." She pointed at the full coat rack. Nothing like hospitality.

Celia was a far cry from Felicity. Felicity had this soft, lovable quality to her, while her mom was prickly. Celia reminded me of a cat that had been provoked, with an arched back and puffed hair. She looked ready to bat her paw at any moment. Her silver-white hair and pale-blue eyes made her look even more cunning.

Felicity made me feel welcome by coming to the entryway and greeting me with a hug. "Thanks for coming, honey."

"I wouldn't miss it. Sorry I'm late. Josh had to kick my butt in hoops." For her I would give an excuse, even if her mother *tsked* about it.

Felicity laughed. "I love that kid."

"Me too."

"Such a shame you'll never have one of your own," Celia said under her breath.

"Mom." Felicity's tight voice said she was obviously embarrassed.

Her mom stomped off without another word. Hallelujah.

Felicity took my hand and led me into the family room, where the festivities were taking place. I recognized a few women, old coworkers and employees of my dad and Ryan. There were also some women Felicity worked with now. Candy and Eden, her sweet sisters-in-law, married to her nice older brothers, Tag and Shawn, were there and all smiles. They both waved and smiled at me. I'm not sure how Celia raised such nice kids. And why did Celia like her daughters-in-law and not my dad? All I had to do was look at fifteen-year-old Claire, Eden's oldest daughter and one of Celia's granddaughters, to take a guess why. Celia had three granddaughters, so it wasn't like she would never have grandchildren. Maybe she somehow thought it would be different if her daughter had one versus her sons. Who knew?

Felicity and I sat down next to each other on two fold-up chairs. The room was decorated in silver and deep green, the wedding colors. My bridesmaid dress was deep green. Yes, I got roped into being another maid of honor, or matron now, since I was married. But at least this time the dress covered all essential parts. It was sleeveless, but floor-length. No Spanx required.

The only drawback was Celia. I couldn't wait for her to tell me I should eat something once in a while like she did at the fitting a few weeks ago. She didn't know me at all— before my little secret I could throw down food like no one's business. It meant I had to run like no one's business to keep it from showing, but I loved food.

Hopefully someday soon I would again. It was getting so serious I had to decline ice cream last night. I had to lie and tell Ryan I had some earlier with Krissy. I lied out of love, which didn't count. And I would tell Ryan the truth in six days.

It was cute to watch Ryan shake his gift and try to figure out what I got him. I had no idea what he got me, but the package was long and thin. No matter what it was, my gift was better.

Felicity kept ahold of my hand for the longest time. It was sweet, but it worried me. It was as if she needed comfort. I was happy to provide it, but I wished things were easier for her.

"Dad said the new furniture arrived for your place." I tried to make light, happy conversation.

"It's beautiful. I can't wait for you to see it," Felicity responded.

"Maybe I can sneak over before we head to the mountains on Tuesday."

"That would be great. I should be there all day tomorrow. I want to paint the hall bath before we leave."

"Did you finally pick a color?"

She grinned. "Hopefully. Jeff is tired of looking at paint samples." She was correct. Dad told her to just pick and if she hated it, they could redo it. "I think I'm going to go with that truffle color I showed you last week."

"I think that will look great."

She squeezed my hand. "We need to get back to our standing lunch dates on Tuesday."

"I'd love that." Well, as soon as I could eat more than pretzels and flat soda.

The lovely moment was gone with the announcement from Candy that it was time to open gifts.

Who would have thought such a sweet thing could be used as a weapon of mass destruction? I was learning in life and in the profession I'd chosen to never underestimate people's ability to turn a positive into a negative. Celia wiped all the joy off Felicity's face when she handed her the first gift and said, "Don't worry about not breaking the bows, we all know how many kids you will have—zero."

I normally kept my mouth shut to keep the peace, but that was uncalled for and a stupid wives' tale. I glared straight into Celia's pale, narrowed eyes. She needed to pluck her eyebrows, by the way. Some chin hairs needed some attention as well.

"You're wrong. She has a daughter."

Silence reigned, and the stares multiplied in my direction, like no one had ever stood up to the woman. I paid them no attention. Instead I looked into the beautiful ice-blue eyes of my soon-to-be stepmother, and the tears of gratitude welling in them made it all worth it.

No one said a word, but the frigid stare from Celia warned me I was asking for trouble. My eyes answered.

Bring it on.

Twelve

RYAN REACHED FOR MY HAND. "Is Maviny texting you again?"

I looked up from my phone and only took his hand for a few seconds. The snowy mountain roads on our drive to Beaver Creek were making me nervous, and I wanted both of his hands on the wheel. I let out a heavy breath.

"She's freaking out because Jay has dropped off the face of the earth." He never responded to my calls, making Maviny think he was dead, so she'd called him and hadn't heard back. "I'm trying to talk her into calling his parents first before she calls the authorities."

"If I were her," my mother-in-law, Kaye, responded from the backseat, "I would thank my lucky stars and move on."

Ryan and I shared a what-the-heck glance. That did not sound like my mother-in-law at all. She'd been behaving oddly ever since we picked her up from the airport yesterday. She didn't even call Guy to let him know she'd made it here. Guy called Ryan to ask last night. When we asked Kaye about it, she played it off like it had slipped her mind.

"He probably just needs some time to think," I defended Jay.

"I've been in those shoes." Ryan squeezed my knee.

It wasn't a fun time for us last year when Ryan wore that pair.

Kaye waved her beautifully manicured hand around. "Oh, please. Ryan Aaron Carter, I hope you thank your lucky stars every day that Charlee stuck around. You men and your thinking. What do you have to think about? Here you are given a fabulous girl, and you do everything you can to ruin it and make her feel like less of a person in the process. You're all idiots."

Ryan and I both sat speechless for a few seconds before Ryan did a quick glance in the rearview mirror. "Mom, is everything all right?"

Kaye took Josh's hand and kissed it. "I'm perfect."

Josh grinned at his grammy and handed her one of the chocolate chip cookies they'd made together last night for the trip.

Kaye happily took the cookie. "Thank you, honey." She bit into that baby and chewed with a vengeance. She polished off a few more all in the same manner. It was kind of scary, so I didn't say anything more.

Some vacation it was turning out to be so far. I had Maviny texting me every half hour asking me what she should do or what she thought was going through Jay's head or if I thought he was dead.

My husband was worried about his ex-wife, who had called yesterday to check in with Josh. Long gone was Victoria's fake cheeriness; she sounded like she had been crying, but she wouldn't admit it to Ryan. Ryan had visions of Maxime becoming Josh's stepfather running through his head, and it was driving him mad. I hated the thought too, but I was trying not to worry about it unless we had to.

But I was worried about the woman in the backseat who was not the sweet mother-in-law I was used to. Sure, Kaye always had some spunk to her, but this wasn't spunky. It was more like resentment. What, or should I say who, was it directed at? Guy was at the top of my culprit list. Were they having marriage troubles? And to top it off, Celia wasn't pleased with my outburst, as she called it, at the wedding shower. She was taking her wrath out on my dad, which had Felicity in tears. What a way to start a wedding and life.

Eloping— or surprise weddings— were the only way to go. I smiled over at my sanity, driving us carefully up to the resort. "I love you." It was all I could think of to say to convey how grateful I was that he was my husband and that we were facing this crazy world together.

His pearly whites came out, and all felt right in the world. "Love you more."

I caught Kaye rolling her eyes in the backseat. That couldn't be good.

Thank goodness for Josh. "Mom, let's sing."

My heart melted. Josh's new name for me got Kaye to smile.

"What should we sing?"

"Felix Naughty Dog!"

"What?" Kaye laughed.

"Just go with it, Mom." It was much more entertaining when he didn't get the words right.

The mood shifted in the car, allowing me to enjoy the scenery, meaning my husband and the beautiful winter view outside of our SUV. The mountains were covered in snow; it clung to everything, including the pine trees. When the sun peeked out from time to time, it made the snow blinding. The roads had been plowed and salted, but there were icy patches. It was slow going even with four-wheel-drive.

Josh serenaded us with every Christmas carol he knew until we arrived in paradise. Beaver Creek had a European flair with cobblestone walks, boutiques, and restaurants that looked straight out of a Swiss Alps village. The crowning jewel was an outdoor ice-skating rink in the center of town. Not to mention the ski resort that shrouded the quaint town. It was heavenly.

Ryan made it more so. He was going native on me and hadn't shaved for a couple of days. I loved his stubble and wanted to kiss his face off, well, as long as his breath was fresh. While unloading the car, Ryan took a minute to remind me why I was so in love with him. He wrapped me up and nuzzled my neck. "You packed the Mrs. Claus dress, right?" he whispered in my ear.

"It depends on how naughty or nice you've been."

"How's this? You and my mom have spa reservations in an hour."

I leaned away from him, so touched by his thoughtfulness. "What?"

"I figured you could use some pampering while I take Josh to his ski lesson."

I crushed my lips against his for a stirring moment. "I brought the dress and heels, by the way." For Ryan I would take the hooker heels out of retirement. I'd had no idea how fond he was of them until a few days ago.

"Mmm." He pulled me as close as he could with our winter coats on. "Merry Christmas to me."

Wow, could he still make the butterflies take flight. It gave me hope that the Christmas vacation I'd dreamed of would still happen.

The sweet moment and my hopes diminished when Ryan pulled out his mom's suitcase. He stared at the sleek black designer luggage.

"Do you think something is going on with my parents?" he whispered so Kaye wouldn't hear. She and Josh were exploring some of the decorated pine trees on the grounds nearby.

I hated to give him anything else to worry about, but… "I think so. Did your dad say anything when you talked to him last night?"

"No, but he cut the conversation short when I asked him how he was."

"Hmmm."

Ryan ran the back of his cold hand down my cool cheek. It was only about thirty degrees outside. "Do you think you could talk to my mom? For some reason, I think she's irritated with me."

I reached up and took his hand. "I don't think it's you, just men in general."

"My dad must have really ticked her off."

"I'll see what I can find out."

"You are the best wife."

"I know."

He planted one chaste kiss on my aching-to-make-out lips. "Are you feeling okay?"

"Why do you keep asking me that?"

"You've had a lot going on, and there is something… different about you."

I tilted my head. "Different how?"

He pressed his lips together and took his I'm-thinking stance. Or more like his I'm-trying-not-to-say-the-wrong-thing stance. "I'm not sure I can put it into words."

That was the safe thing to say.

I leaned into him, placing my hands on his chest, and stole a longer kiss. "Don't worry about me. I'm good, we're good."

He wrapped me up in his arms. "You are very good."

Our husband-wife time was over when Kaye and Josh appeared to help with the luggage and gifts. It was probably a good thing. The butterflies were chanting for some major displays of public affection, and they almost got their way. We would save their plans for a more private time.

We got checked in and settled in our gorgeous suite, complete with a Christmas tree that looked like it came straight from the North Pole. There was even a fireplace for us to hang our stockings on. Red and green glass ornaments filled the tree, which was wrapped with silk, red-wired ribbon. My poorly wrapped gifts under the designer tree looked out of place, but I reminded myself all that wrapping paper would be in the trash in four days.

Kaye and I parted ways with our boys. Josh was excited to hit the slopes, and I needed a nap and planned to take one on the massage table. I had the best husband ever. It's almost as if he knew. But he didn't, did he? His question by the car had me wondering.

We ran into my dad and Felicity. They were checking in along with all of Felicity's family. Mother, brothers, wives, and children. I was hoping to avoid everyone until after the spa, but surprise.

I went the safe route and hugged Dad in the lobby. "Hi, Daddy."

He kissed my head. "Hey, baby girl. Where are you headed off to?"

"The spa."

"Sounds lovely." Felicity hugged my mother-in-law. "How are you, Kaye? We're so happy you could make it to the wedding."

Kaye took a deep breath and put on a strained smile. "I wouldn't want to be anywhere else." That sounded partially true. Kaye loved her kids and grandchildren, but there was a lie in there.

Celia was squinting her eyes and scrunching her face at me from across the lobby. I wasn't even to going to bat an eye at her snotty stare. I looked on the bright side. The more she did that, the more wrinkles she would get, so it hurt her more than me. Felicity's brothers were looking around the posh lobby in wonder. It matched our suite, but on a grander scale. Felicity's three nieces, ages fifteen to seven, were all there. Super cute girls. Let's pray they turned out like their aunt. The seven-year-old, Sofia, was the flower girl and would be walking down the aisle with Josh. Candy and Eden, the sisters-in-law, were waving at me and giving me toothy grins. I liked them. I waved back and made a mental note to try and spend some time with them.

I watched Kaye look longingly at Dad and Felicity when they walked off together hand in hand toward the check-in counter. A wistful sigh escaped her.

I strung my arm through my elegant mother-in-law's arm. "Mom, is something going on with you and Dad?"

She patted my hand. "No. Not a thing." That sounded as if it had a double meaning.

"Are you sure? Do you want to talk?"

"All I want to do is enjoy the afternoon with you."

The nap didn't happen while the masseuse tried to work out the knots in my back. All I could think about was my in-laws. I thought back to the last time we saw them together at our wedding in June. Guy was affectionate and attentive to Kaye. They wore the mark of a couple that had been through the thick and thin of life. It made their bond strong and deep. Nothing seemed amiss. But now something was definitely up.

Kaye made lots of small talk while we got pedicures, never allowing me an in to find out what was going on. She caught me up on our nieces we never saw. Evan didn't have the best of relationships with his baby mamas— one flat-out refused to let anyone from our side have contact with her child. But Kaye did her best to be in her granddaughters' lives. Next, she told me all about the Christmas tea party she coordinated over the weekend, anything not to talk about Guy.

Just when she took a breath and I was going to sneak in a question about Guy, Candy and Eden walked in all smiles.

"Do you mind if we join you?" Eden asked.

"Not at all."

Candy and Eden took the two empty pedicure chairs next to me. They were both around Felicity's age, maybe a little older. Down-to-earth described them well, both with easy-to-style, short hair and mom jeans and sweaters. You would have thought they were blood related.

"Candy and Eden, this is my mother-in-law, Kaye. She's from the D.C. area."

Kaye was all smiles. "It's so nice to meet you."

Candy and Eden shared the sentiment before choosing the type of pedicure they wanted. Kaye and I were already well into ours. I was getting a fantastic foot massage at the moment. It almost made me forget I felt like puking. Morning sickness was a myth. This was an all-day, every-freaking-day kind of sickness. I knew it would be worth it in the end, but holy crap was it kicking my butt.

Once Candy and Eden were situated with feet soaking, they turned their attention back toward me. They wore these strange looks of admiration. At first it kind of wigged me out, until Candy said, "Can I just say thank you?"

"For what?"

"For standing up to Celia."

"You're our hero." Eden's face lit up.

"It was brilliant," Candy gushed.

I bit my lip. "I'm afraid it only made more problems for my dad and Felicity."

Candy waved her hand. "There's no pleasing her."

"Oh, so it's not just my dad?"

"Are you kidding me? Since the day Shawn brought me home to meet her, I've never pleased her," Eden admitted.

Candy raised her hand. "Same here. I've never been good enough for Tag, according to her."

"Have Tag or Shawn ever said anything to her?"

They both laughed.

"They're Momma's boys." Eden wasn't pleased.

"Men," Kaye *tsked.*

Candy and Eden nodded to agree with Kaye's obvious distaste for the opposite sex at the moment.

"I like Ryan," I threw in for good measure.

"Newlyweds." Eden laughed off my defense of the male species.

"Just wait." Candy joined in laughing.

"For what?"

"The moment you roll over in bed and think, I hate this man's guts, and why did I ever get married?" Eden was obviously speaking from experience.

My eyebrows hit my bangs. "Love is a choice."

Kaye reached for my hand. "Some days are harder than others to make that choice."

"Oh, don't get me wrong. I love Shawn, but believe me, give it a few years, and there will come a day you will think twice about your choice to get married."

I didn't respond to Eden. I couldn't imagine feeling that way about Ryan. My focus was on the woman who held my hand and whose eyes said she was having second thoughts. I wanted to know what was going on, but I couldn't ask in front of Eden and Candy.

Thankfully the tide of the conversation turned to the ski conditions and how beautiful Beaver Creek was.

I would have liked to say I left completely refreshed and invigorated, but besides feeling all pregnant, I was more than worried now about my in-laws. And just when I thought things couldn't get any more interesting, two people I didn't expect to see came walking into the lobby.

I stood by the massive Christmas tree in the lobby in shock. Saying that things were going to get interesting was a colossal understatement.

"Mom? Jay?"

Thirteen

KAYE HADN'T NOTICED THE NEW arrivals, so she kept walking, not stopping until she heard my mom call my name.

"CJ, honey, surprise!"

Oh, surprise didn't even cover it.

Mom dropped her luggage and rushed to me with arms open wide. She embraced me like it was old times. Times I'd missed.

I allowed myself to sink against her. "Mom, what are you doing here?"

She held on tighter. "I've missed you, honey, and I couldn't stand the thought of spending one more Christmas apart."

She sounded sincere, but I stepped back to loosen her hold on me. She looked fantastic. Not sure what she had been doing since June, but it was working. She was always beautiful to me, but her new layered cut went fabulously with her gray-streaked, brown hair, and she looked svelte. And more than anything, she looked happy. Like, happier than I'd seen her in years.

"I've missed you too, but Mom, this is, you know…"

She pulled me in for another bear hug. "So, your dad is getting married. He won't even know I'm here."

I was pretty sure he was going to notice. "Did you get a room?"

"I figured I could stay with you. Jay, here, got the only room they had available through the holidays."

Jay sheepishly approached, and Kaye entered the mix too.

Kaye and my mom embraced like the old friends and neighbors they were.

"The kids' suite is plenty big. We can share a bedroom. Is that all right, sweetie?" Kaye flashed a smile at me.

I lost all function to speak or move. How was this happening? It didn't matter one way or another if I gave my approval.

"I'll show you to our room so you can get settled," Kaye informed my mom.

They skipped off like schoolgirls, leaving me behind still fumbling for words.

So many words were running through my mind, but I couldn't articulate even one. All I kept thinking was moms, both of our moms were here. And Dad. Dad was here. Dad was getting married. Now my ex-boyfriend was here. Moms were staying in our suite. That meant Josh would have to stay on the couch, which translated into Josh staying in our bed. That was going to mean an unhappy Ryan. He had plans for that Mrs. Claus dress tonight. Like detailed, I've-been-texting-my-wife-making-her-blush kind of plans. The butterflies were quite excited.

Jay shook me out of my thoughts. "Charlee." Jay stood

leaning on his right leg. It was his signature stance. The All-American boy was looking unsure. He ran his fingers through his sandy blonde hair. "You're probably wondering what your mom and I are doing here."

Yes, yes, I was.

"It's a funny story. Do you want to sit down? You look…" He studied me.

"What?" I found my voice.

"Different."

My eyebrow raised. Weird how Ryan had said the same thing. Does pregnancy make you look different?

"It's a good different."

"Uh-huh. We'd better sit down before you talk yourself into some trouble."

He laughed nervously and led the way to a couple of the chairs near the fireplace in the lobby. We sat next to each other but not too close. We were still friends, but I think a weirdness would always exist between us since once upon a time he wanted to marry me.

"Thanks for returning my phone calls, by the way," I jabbed at him.

He leaned forward and rested his hands on his knees, avoiding eye contact with me. "About that."

"Yeah, about that. What's going on, Jay? Ignoring phone calls and people isn't like you."

He let out a heavy breath. "I know. I just needed some time to think."

"You had Maviny worried sick. She thought you were dead."

He sat up and smiled. "Sounds like her."

"So, what have you been thinking about?"

"Maviny. You."

"Me?"

"It's not what you think."

"Okay. Enlighten me."

"I love Maviny."

"Tell me something I don't know."

"She drives me crazy."

I wasn't surprised, but it made me laugh. "Crazy isn't necessarily a bad thing." I knew some of the things I did drove Ryan crazy. Sometimes he drove me crazy.

"Most of the time I love it, but she's kind of intense. And we're different."

"Differences can be good things."

"I suppose."

"What differences have you worried?"

He sat back in his chair and relaxed some. "She's a girl."

"Umm… I would think that would be a plus for you."

He laughed. "I definitely enjoy that part, but you know what I mean. She's a girly girl. She can't stand it if one hair is out of place, and her idea of roughing it is a three-star hotel. I tried taking her camping and fishing. She fell into the lake and almost threw up when she saw me hook the worm."

He had me smiling. "But did she stay?"

He turned thoughtful. "Yeah, she did, and she tried to fish until she got the hook stuck in her hair with the worm on it."

"Sounds like you had a good time."

"We did."

"So what's your real problem?"

His chest rose and fell. "You were easy, Charlee."

"Oh, really?" I knew what he meant but loved seeing him turn a few shades of red.

"Not that kind of easy. You are the Sunday-morning kind of easy. Laid back, comfortable. Maviny is a Friday night, exciting and exhausting."

"But Maviny's feelings for you have to add more comfort to your relationship than I ever gave you."

"I'm over you, Charlee."

"I wasn't worried."

He patted my knee in a friendly gesture. "I'm happy you're happy. It's written all over your face. I knew I was never enough for you, and I worry Maviny will end up feeling the same way."

"Jay." I rested my hand on his. "You were exactly what I needed at the time. The way I felt had nothing to do with you. You were more than enough and still are. It was me that wasn't enough for you. I couldn't give you what you deserved. Maviny can and does. She has a terrible way of showing it, but she wanted you to ask her to stay. She wanted more of you, not less."

His eyes lit up. "I want more of her too, but when she told me about the opportunity in Ireland, I didn't want to hold her back."

"I think you two need to talk."

"That's why I'm here."

"Why are you with my mom?"

"I told you it was a funny story. I ran into her

yesterday at the mall in Overland Park; we were both doing some Christmas shopping. We got to talking about Maviny, and she basically told me I was a moron, but she realized she was just like me. She misses you, Charlee."

My eyes misted.

"She decided we'd better do something about how dumb we've been."

"On a whim, you decided to drive all the way up here from Kansas?"

"Yeah, kind of."

"Why didn't you tell Maviny?"

He shrugged. "I don't know. I thought maybe if I was here when she showed up it would be kind of romantic."

"It's not a bad thought. I'll keep your secret."

"Thanks. And I hope having your mom here doesn't cause too many problems."

"I hope so too. Where's Mark?"

"Charlee," my favorite voice interrupted.

"Mom!" my other favorite voice came barreling toward me in his ski get-up, including helmet and goggles. He had the biggest grin on his face.

His daddy wasn't smiling at all. He lasered in on Jay. Jay, in a flash, stood up.

Josh landed in my arms. His cheeks were red from the cold, but he was beaming. "Mom, I was awesome!"

I wrapped Josh up and sat him on my lap to warm him up, while my other guy marked his territory. Ryan landed next to me and went in for the kill. He leaned down and kissed me. He lingered longer than a regular hello kiss.

"Hi," I was able to get in when his lips departed.

"Hey there." He pecked my lips for good measure.

I smirked at him.

"What are you doing here, Jay?" No hi or pleasantries from my husband.

Jay was polite and held out his hand to shake Ryan's. "I'm here to see Maviny. How are you?"

Ryan shook Jay's hand. "Never better."

"I'm happy to hear that. I'll let you enjoy your wife and son. I need to check in."

Ryan's smile said, "Don't let me keep you."

"We'll talk later. I'll help you prep for Maviny's arrival tomorrow," I called out to a retreating Jay.

Jay waved and laughed while walking toward the check-in counter.

As soon as Jay was out of ear shot, Ryan took Jay's vacated seat. "What was all that about, and why was your hand touching his?"

"If I didn't know better I would think you were jealous. Or maybe you don't trust me?"

"I trust you. Him not so much."

I didn't get to explain. Josh was demanding our attention. "Mom, you should have seen me. I can do the pizza and the airplane!"

I looked at Ryan to explain. "That's what the instructors call making a wedge with his skis and his stance for balance."

"Gotcha." I started to take off Josh's helmet. "I'm proud of you, big guy."

"I don't want to take off my helmet or goggles."

"Why?"

"Because I look cool."

Ryan and I laughed at him.

"Okay, Mr. Cool. Let's get you in the tub before dinner."

"Can I wear my helmet and goggles in there?"

"I don't think so, buddy," Ryan gave it to him straight.

Josh dramatically draped himself across me in protest. Sometimes we were so mean.

I guessed this was a good time to break the news. "So, Jay didn't come alone."

Ryan cocked his head. "I thought Maviny wasn't coming until tomorrow."

"She's not. There's been a fun twist in the plot. My mom's here."

Ryan's eyes about popped out of his head. "But your dad is…"

"I know. And more fun, she's staying in our suite."

Never had a man looked so disappointed. "We'll get another room."

"Jay booked the last room available through the holidays."

Ryan's look said he wanted to punch Jay more now than ever. "We're going to need a vacation from our vacation."

Fourteen

I TRIED TO CONTACT MY dad before he ran into my mom, but he and Felicity were out skiing and doing whatever else engaged couples do. I was on a no-need-to-know basis and planned on keeping it that way. Dad was smart and turned off his phone. But like all men, he was bound to get hungry and, unfortunately, it was at the same time everyone else in our suite— except me— did too. I shouldn't say I wasn't hungry. I just felt like if I ate I would die, so it kind of put a damper on the whole eating thing.

The resort had two restaurants; one was more high-end. The wedding rehearsal dinner would take place there. The other one was still on the fancy-schmancy side, but pretty much everywhere in Beaver Creek was, and it had been a long day, so we hit the closest thing to us. The "lower" class one.

My mom was all of a sudden my mom. She was fawning all over me and telling me how beautiful I was and how proud she was of all my accomplishments, even though I had gotten a B in my psychopathology class. I was doing my best not to let my first B get to me, but I may have shed a tear. I was blaming it on the pregnancy. I tried to ask her about Mark, but she waved it off and said he was spending the holiday with his kids in Kansas, like it was no big deal. This was all so weird.

Ryan held my hand while we walked through the lobby behind our moms, who had Josh in the middle of them. They were doting on him like grandmothers do, and Josh was lapping up the attention. Something seemed so off about all of this. I was sure earlier in our suite while we were getting ready I heard the mothers in the other room trash-talking men and giggling as if they were in high school.

Ryan was in a funk too. Besides his mom not opening up to us, Josh wanted to call his mommy to tell her about his day in ski school and on the slopes, but when Ryan tried, she didn't answer. Where Josh was concerned, she always picked up on the first ring even if it was the middle of the night where she was. Ryan had unfounded thoughts of Victoria and Maxime eloping or Maxime not allowing her to answer the phone. Ryan must have called ten times, leaving a message each time that Josh wanted to speak to her. He kept checking his phone to see if she'd called.

"I'm sure she's fine and still single. She's probably sleeping and didn't turn up the volume on her phone."

He placed his phone back in his pocket and squeezed my hand. "You're right. I'm sorry I've been so distracted."

I focused on our moms. "There is plenty of distraction to go around."

He wrapped his arm around me and whispered in my ear, "Hey, my focus is on my super sexy wife, whom I meant to tell how amazing she looks in those jeans."

"You're looking fantastic in yours as well. Too bad that's all I'm going to see you in at this rate."

He groaned against my ear. "At least we don't have any more moms."

"There's that."

"I plan to steal you away tomorrow, just you and me."

"And what are we going to do?"

"I was thinking we should hit the slopes and do a few runs. And then make use of the outdoor hot tub. I made sure to pack your bikini."

He was killing me. Those were two big things on the not-to-do list for someone in my condition. He had no idea how much I wanted to do both with him, but I refused to do anything that would harm the secret I carried. I turned to him, grabbed his sweater, and peered adoringly into his eyes. This was my classic move to get what I wanted.

"So… I was thinking we should try this little place in the village where we can make our own pottery." I had a slew of excuses at my disposal. I had been doing my research.

Ryan had never made this look before. It was a mix of did-I-hear-her-right and is-this-really-my-wife. "Since when have you been into pottery?"

I so wasn't, but I looked up things to do as a couple in Beaver Creek, and that popped up. "It's the *it* thing to do as a couple."

"Is that so?" He grinned.

"Uh-huh." I leaned in to secure the deal with a kiss, but like all my other plans of late, it died a fiery death. My parents had the worst freaking timing.

"Monica?" Dad's shock rang through the lobby. We had almost made it to the restaurant.

I took a deep breath and turned around, making sure to take Ryan's hand. I needed his steady presence for the four-alarm fire in progress.

Dad and Felicity stood ten feet away from the moms. Josh was running to my dad and hugging his legs, bursting to tell him about his skiing experience. He loved his grandpa Jeff. Dad, on autopilot, put his arm around Josh, but his eyes were glued on his ex-wife. Felicity wore a look of insecurity and incredulity. Felicity leaned more into Dad.

My gorgeous mom, who looked like she'd had a makeover, was all smiles. "Jeff, Felicity, how nice to see you. Congratulations. You must be excited about the big day on Friday."

Dad and Felicity stood dumbfounded.

My mom didn't miss a beat. She took a few steps toward me and reached for my free hand, pulling me away from Ryan and toward her. "I hope you don't mind me crashing the party, Jeff, but I couldn't miss another Christmas with our girl."

Dad struggled for what to say. He looked at me for guidance while Felicity's grip on his arm looked more like a tourniquet now. I could see Felicity comparing herself to my mom. I felt awful for her. She already felt like my mom's shadow loomed over a good portion of their relationship.

While Dad tried to form words and the world stood still in this unreal reality we had all fallen into, I decided to take matters into my own hands. Mom and I needed to talk, and, unlike my mother-in-law, she was going to tell me exactly what was going on. "You know, Mom and I are going to do some shopping and have dinner in the village." I didn't think I could eat right then anyway. Not only was the baby having its way with me, but this whole freakish event was getting to my appetite.

Dad never could get anything out, but I could tell Felicity was hoping he would make my mom vanish. Ryan, on the other hand, let out a sigh loud enough to blow up that inflatable snow globe we had in our front yard. This was not the romantic holiday getaway we had envisioned. It was more like a holiday horror show, and we had front row, center stage seats to it.

Ryan kissed my cheek as I walked by, pulling my mom along with me. I felt bad leaving him to deal with what I knew was going to be a dinner filled with either awkward silence or uncomfortable conversation. Probably some of both.

I pulled Mom through the lobby, not thinking about the fact that it was in the twenties outside and I was only wearing a sweater. What was some frigid weather compared to taking the heat off my dad?

I stayed close to Mom to share body heat as we made our way across the plaza, passed the adorable outdoor ice-skating rink, to a snazzy eatery that played live music at night. Ryan and I talked about going one of these nights. I wasn't counting on it. Knowing our luck as of late, we would sneak away only to slip on the ice and break an ankle or something. Thankfully, no broken bones happened on our trek. But it was so cold that breathing in hurt. That meant no talking until we reached the warm eatery.

The hostess thought nothing of our lack of winter outerwear. This was Colorado, after all. Most guys on campus wore shorts and parkas throughout the winter, and those "Ski Naked" T-shirts weren't just a fun slogan.

I waited to say anything significant to Mom until we were seated in a cozy booth, farthest from where the indie band was playing. There's nothing like reggae Christmas carols.

With my ginger ale with no ice ordered and a quick scan of the menu, I zeroed in on the woman smiling like nothing was out of the ordinary.

"Why are you really here, Mom?" I got straight to business. I was afraid, given our last several years, a question like that would set her off, but she kept on surprising me.

She reached across for both of my hands. She rubbed them warm like I did for Josh after we played basketball together in the cold. "I miss you."

"I miss you too, but why now? Why Dad's wedding?"

"Honestly, this has nothing to do with your father. I needed to see you."

Worst-case scenarios ran through my pregnant brain. "Is something wrong?"

Her eyes shone with unshed tears. "No. For the first time in a long time, things are right. I'm right."

"Explain."

Her grip on my hands tightened. "I've been seeing a therapist."

My eyebrows hit my hairline. This was the woman who was adamantly against me majoring in psychology and thought being a CPA was a better career choice.

She laughed. "I know it's shocking."

"You could say that."

"I woke up a few months ago and realized how miserable and lonely I was."

"Are you and Mark having problems?"

She pressed her lips together and took a second to answer. "We are, but it goes beyond that. All my life I've tried to fix my problems by not confronting them, or with temporary fixes like retail therapy, alcohol, or even men once I left your father." Her cheeks weren't rosy from the cold. "It's easier to blame other people that way."

Who was this woman, and what had she done with my mother?

Our server brought us our drinks and took our order. All that sounded good to me was bread, so I ordered a basket of their fresh baked rolls. The server and my mom both gave scrutinizing glances, but I wasn't making any excuses or apologies for it. I needed some nourishment, and I needed to not throw it all back up. Thankfully, Mom ordered a non-smelly salad.

Mom took my hands back up again. There was such softness to her features. I couldn't remember the last time she looked so warm and inviting.

"I know I did my best to push you away, CJ."

Tears stung my eyes.

"I was so unhappy after the divorce, I couldn't even be happy about the best thing that ever happened to me.

This makes me sound like a terrible mother, but I was jealous of you. I've never known who I was or who I am. But you have always known who you are, and you've never let anyone tell you differently, not even me or your dad. I love how you do things your own way."

"Even though you didn't get to pick out my wedding dress?" I smiled.

"Well, maybe that bothered me."

"What does all this mean to you, to us?"

"My therapist says when our actions are out of harmony with our desires and who we really are or want to be, it causes friction in every aspect of our lives."

"Sounds like a smart therapist."

"She reminds me of a girl I love."

I wasn't used to compliments from her, but I would take them.

"More than anything she's helped me look to myself to find happiness, and you know what I discovered?"

I shook my head no.

"You."

"Me?"

She reached up and wiped some of the tears that spilled over. "Honey, the best thing I've ever done is be your mother, even though I've done a poor job of it the last several years. I'm done missing out on the important moments and all the small ones in between. That's why when I ran into Jay, I decided I wasn't going to let another minute pass by before I did something about it. I know the timing isn't the greatest, but really, I'm over your dad. I'll always love him for giving me you. And maybe there will always be a part of me that will wonder what would have happened if I'd stayed. But his affair wasn't our only problem, and I can't look back now and second guess myself. All I can do now is move forward and fix me. You are part of me, and I need us to be better."

"I want that too." I was full-on bawling.

Our server interrupted with our food. Poor guy was in and out in a flash to not get caught up in some emotional female thing.

Mom grinned at my bread and ginger ale. "You know, when I was pregnant with you, I used to eat plain baked potatoes to help with morning sickness."

I dropped the piece of bread I had picked up.

"Don't look so surprised. I still know my girl."

I was shocked but honestly relieved. Now I had someone to talk to about the weird things going on in my body. Better yet, it was my mom. "Please don't say anything to anyone. Ryan doesn't know. I was planning on telling him Christmas morning."

"I promise to keep my grandbaby a secret."

"I love the sound of that. Grandbaby."

"Besides you, I couldn't ask for a better Christmas present."

Fifteen

RYAN RAN THE BACK OF his hand down my cheek as we lay in the dark of our room listening to our moms next door talk and giggle like they were at a slumber party. Josh was fast asleep, tucked into me with his head resting on my chest.

Ryan's eyes drifted toward Josh. "I love how you love our son."

Those dang tears found a way out again. What was this baby doing to my tear ducts? "That's the first time you've ever called him *ours.*"

Ryan got as close he could, making it a Josh sandwich. He brushed my lips with his. "I didn't mean to make you cry. Are you sure everything is okay? I thought you said you had a great time with your mom."

I did, but it gave me so much to think about. "Do you ever think you're going to wake up, roll over, look at me, and think, 'I hate her guts'?"

Even in the dark I could see his pretty green eyes double in size. "Why would you even ask a question like that?"

"Felicity's sister-in-law said it was normal. And my parents are divorced, my mom and Mark are on the rocks, your parents are obviously having issues. My mom confirmed our suspicions there but wouldn't tell me anything your mom confided in her; she thought it wasn't her place. But listen to the two of them. They're obviously having a man-hating session next door."

I was catching bits and pieces of what they were saying about men being so clueless and how they didn't appreciate a thing. That all men cared about were themselves. I drowned them out and focused back on Ryan. "I don't want to wake up in twenty years and hate you or have you hate me."

Ryan pressed his lips against mine, making me relax. "Breathe, Charlee," he whispered, "I could never hate you."

"You don't know that. Do you think our parents when they got married ever thought they would hate each other?"

"They're not us. And I do know what's it's like to wake up and hate the person lying next to me. I won't do it again. Aren't you the one who always tells me that we choose to love?"

I nodded.

"You're my choice. Every day, Charlee. I know we'll have our own problems; but I love you, and we'll work them out. And even if you woke up one day and told me you hated me, I'd tell you to get over it because I'm not letting you go."

I smiled and kissed him. "Sorry for being so dramatic, but this trip is nothing like I imagined it would be."

"You're telling me. Our son stole my favorite spot."

"Maybe instead of making pottery tomorrow, we can sneak back to our suite alone."

"Mmm." He nuzzled my neck. "Now you're talking."

"Let's just hope no other unexpected visitors show up."

"Who else could there be?"

Oh. That was the wrong question to ask. It was like Ryan was begging fate, and fate said hold my beer and watch this.

We were woken up in the middle of the night by Ryan's phone violently vibrating. Ryan untangled himself from Josh and me.

"Does she know what time it is here?" he grumbled before answering. The bedside clock read 3:42.

Josh shifted against me but didn't wake up.

I figured it was Victoria returning Ryan's slew of messages from yesterday. I kissed Josh's head, expecting to go right back to sleep after Ryan told Victoria he would call her back later. That was a nice thought.

Ryan sat up and ran his fingers through his hair. Though only a sliver of light came through the door, I could tell something wasn't right. As Ryan listened, his breaths became heavier and deeper.

I placed Josh on Ryan's pillow and sat up. I placed my hand on Ryan's arm, trying to lend him some comfort.

Finally he spoke. "You should have called before you made this decision."

I had never heard Ryan be so harsh with her. My first thought was that she eloped. My stomach churned at the thought of Maxime being Josh's stepfather. But I should have known that was out of Victoria's character to do something, well, something I would do. I thought back to her fussy, bedazzled wedding to Ryan. I'm sure if she ever remarried, she would have another stuffy ceremony. No, Victoria did something none of us saw coming. Not sure why. It fit this vacation to the tee. I mean, this way we had the full set of freaking exes along.

"Our suite number is 201. Don't knock. I'll meet you at the door." Ryan hung up and threw his phone on the bed. He rubbed his face in his hands. "She's here."

"I got that. Why?"

"Don't know. She could barely get out that she was here between her sobbing."

"Do you think Maxime hurt her?"

Ryan's tense shoulders dropped. "I didn't even think about that. I guess I'd better get up. She was in the lobby when she called."

"Next time we go on vacation, we aren't telling anyone where we're going."

"Truer words have never been spoken." Ryan jumped out of bed and threw on a T-shirt.

I decided I should probably greet our uninvited guest even though my stomach went from churning to turning. The baby wasn't going to let me forget who was the boss of my body right now. As long as Ryan didn't breathe on me I should be fine. Well, as fine as you could be when your husband's ex-wife crashes your vacation.

What was Kaye going to do when she woke up? She hated her ex-daughter-in-law. Maybe Victoria would be gone by then. I mean, she wasn't planning on staying here, right? She could just go back to Loveland. So maybe we would let her rest; she had to be exhausted. I couldn't believe she'd flown all the way back from Europe and then driven up here. Or maybe she caught a shuttle from the airport in Denver; but that didn't seem her style. I didn't see Victoria using public transportation.

I leaned against Ryan, waiting for the ex-wife to appear. Waves of agitation rolled off him. I'm not sure I had ever seen him so on edge. How he knew when Victoria was on the other side of the door I had no idea, but he opened the door as soon as she landed there.

She was in the same emotional state as when she had dropped off Josh, but she didn't look so physically put together. She actually had some hairs out of place in her topknot, and her jacket was wrinkled. I evilly thought I should snap a picture for posterity, but her tear-stained cheeks and puffy red eyes looked too pathetic. My thoughts went from evil to, honestly, feeling sorry for her. If she would have let me, I might have hugged her. It looked like she could use it.

But she steeled herself and stood up straight, taking a deep breath, trying to stave off her shuddering. "I need to see Josh." She let herself in.

Ryan grabbed her luggage before shutting the door.

We all stood in the entryway, staring at each other in the glow of the nearby Christmas tree.

"Josh is asleep," Ryan informed Victoria of what should have been obvious.

"Where's his room?"

"He's staying in our room, since both of our moms are using his." Ryan's tone said she'd better not even ask to go in our room.

Victoria's eyes begged to question why our moms were here, but she wasn't going to get an answer at the moment. It was too long and convoluted.

"Why don't you sit down," I offered her. She looked dead on her feet.

"I want to see Josh." She wasn't going to let it go.

"We'll bring him out to you. You can both rest on the couch together." I figured she needed him.

Ryan without delay went to our room to pick up the connecting piece in each of our lives.

"Can I get you anything?"

Victoria's first reaction was to squint her blue eyes, but then she started to cry again and asked for some water.

"Sit down. I'll grab you a bottle of water." I headed for the kitchen in our suite. I watched her and, like a child, she sat on the couch and curled into a ball. I wondered what story she was keeping hidden.

Ryan and I came back to her at the same time. He with the love of our lives and me with water. Ryan placed our sleeping angel on Victoria's lap as soon as she was ready to receive him. She clung to him with all she had. I set the bottle down on the coffee table before grabbing the extra bedding in the closet.

Meanwhile, Ryan stood watching his ex-wife and child. He was at a loss for what to say. And I think it was better if we said nothing at all until Victoria was ready to talk. I wasn't sure if she would open up to us. But she was here, and that had to have been a tough choice for her to make.

I set a blanket and pillow near her. "Let us know if you need anything."

She paid us no attention. She only kissed her son's head and cheeks.

I took Ryan's hand and led him back to our bedroom. He followed but kept looking back at the scene in the living area.

When we were behind closed doors, Ryan took me into his arms and held me like he hadn't in a long time, not since our dating days when he felt the weight of the world on his shoulders trying to keep everyone happy and me and Josh in his life.

"Have I mentioned lately how much you mean to me?"

I nodded against him. He was never short on affection in words or action.

"I love you, Charlee."

I loved him more than anything, but he needed to quit breathing on me.

Sixteen

GOING BACK TO SLEEP WAS a joke. Ryan and I lay in bed thinking up all the reasons why Victoria was here and not with her uppity-up boyfriend in Europe. Ryan had never seen her like this. He said she'd never even shed a tear when they got divorced. Ouch. Not that I was complaining. Well, except for his breath.

Three more days of torture. I was putting breath mints in Ryan's stocking. I almost told him about the baby while lying in his arms. I wanted to take his mind off all the troubles that had followed us on vacation. But I stopped myself. I wanted him to be in the right frame of mind when I rocked his world. A Charlee-Ryan original was in the works.

At 6:00 we called it good and got up to get ready. We figured we'd better get out there before the moms. This was going to be fun to explain. I wasn't surprised that they hadn't woken up when Victoria arrived. They'd taken a bottle of wine with them to the bedroom and were up past us. I'm not sure anything good came of it. I just prayed, for Ryan's sake, whatever it was his parents were dealing with could be worked out.

To be honest, I could go either way with Mom and Mark. I was never a huge Mark fan, but I was a big fan of commitment and marriage and thought they both deserved consideration. Mom mentioned, though, that life with Mark meant doing what Mark wanted. And when I asked her if she loved him, she couldn't exactly say. I knew he wasn't happy about her leaving him for Christmas. But I had to admit, I was kind of glad she came, even if the timing was crappy.

Ryan mentioned last night how uncomfortable dinner had been with my dad and Felicity. From what Ryan said, it was apparent Felicity was not happy about my dad's lack of verbal skills. I guessed she also accused him of ogling his ex-wife. By all accounts, Dad vehemently denied it. I had tried to call Dad last night to fill him in on why Mom came, but he didn't answer. I didn't take it as a good sign. I wasn't looking forward to facing them this morning. Or Celia. I could only imagine the heyday she was having with this.

For right now, though, I had another ex-wife to worry about.

I showered, threw up my hair, and put on some asset-flaunting jeans and a figure-flattering sweater. I wanted to wear all my sexy clothes before I couldn't anymore. I wondered when I would start showing. Not soon, at this rate. I felt like I hadn't eaten a decent meal in weeks.

Ryan and I appeared together. It was safer that way. No telling who or what would be lurking on this holiday nightmare, I mean adventure.

We found Victoria and Josh both lying on the couch.

Josh was securely wrapped in his mother's arms and just starting to stir. Victoria was wide awake, peering at her son as if he held the answer to what troubled her. She paid no attention to us.

When Josh was awake enough, he popped up. "Mommy!"

Victoria gave a rare smile. Smiles that were only for Josh. Victoria sat up and refused to let him go.

Ryan and I approached and took the love seat nearby.

"Mom and Dad, Mommy's here." Josh thought he was telling us something we didn't know. We rolled with it.

"Isn't that fun?" I tried my best to act like I meant it.

Ryan said nothing.

"You can see me ski now." Josh was ready to jump out of his mom's arms. He liked to play hard from morning until night.

"How about breakfast first, buddy," Ryan suggested.

Josh must have liked the idea. He wiggled out of Victoria's arms, ready to start his day. We would have to go out for breakfast. Ryan and I had decided this would be a no-cooking kind of vacation. We should have said no exes, but we assumed that was implied.

I was getting ready to get up to help Josh get his clothes and make him presentable for the day when Victoria threw me a curve ball.

"Charlee, do you think we could go for a walk and talk?"

I fell back down next to Ryan, who was as stunned as me. He looked catatonic.

Victoria's eyes pleaded with me, and that was saying something right there.

"Sure. There's a walking track in the gym here." It was a good excuse not to eat, and I was pretty much dying to know why she was there.

I thought for sure she would want to freshen up, maybe put on a pantsuit or something, but she went as-is in her wrinkled clothes and untidy hair. It was a cold day in Satan's paradise when I was more put together than the Victoria's Secret model.

The track hovered above the gym. Only one other person was using it, a man who ran like a pro, just like my husband. We walked a lap, ignoring the runner who circled us three times, before a word was said. I wasn't going to push, and I knew she was uncomfortable. If my practicum had taught me anything, it was that the truth would never reveal itself unless the patient felt comfortable in doing so. Sometimes it took several sessions to accomplish that. I would walk as many laps as needed, or until this baby told me to stop. Baby JC, short for Jensen-Carter as I was referring to him or her, would have the final say.

"You're probably wondering what I'm doing here."

"Yep." I smiled, trying to keep the mood light.

She clammed up for another half lap.

I waited.

"You're not my first choice of people to talk to, but you'll do."

"Since we are being honest, you might want to try to be nice, under the circumstances."

She stopped and met my eyes. She had about two inches on me. "You're right."

Did anyone hear that? Victoria said I was right. I wished I could have recorded it. Her face said that even she couldn't believe she'd said it.

"Now that that's settled. What's wrong?"

She put one foot in front of the other, watching each step of her designer boots. "Everything."

"That narrows it down."

A tiny laughed escaped her.

"You should laugh and smile more often."

"I'm not sure if I know how."

"What do you mean?"

"Do you know what it's like to have to be perfect all the time?" She spoke to her toes.

"No. Why do you feel that pressure?"

"Expectations from family, myself."

"Can you be more specific?"

Her thoughtful eyes decided I was worthy of a glance. "Take, for instance, why I married Ryan."

This was going to be interesting. I'd always wanted to know.

"When we met, everyone said we were perfect for each other. He was successful and handsome. We looked good together. And I was getting closer to thirty than I cared to admit and not married, so I kept seeing him. And then I got…"

"Pregnant."

"I figured Ryan would tell you."

"It's nothing to be embarrassed about."

"Tell that to my parents. They said I had to get married, to think of how it would look. So, I got married and then lost the baby, but I felt guilty because I was relieved no one would know Ryan had to marry me."

"He told me himself that he wanted to marry you."

She shrugged. "Maybe. I think if we had given it some time we would have broken up. But once we were married, I felt trapped."

"Did you love him at all?"

"I loved the idea of us. We were perfect together."

"No, you weren't. There's no such thing."

"Everyone thought we were." Her snippy voice was back.

"Not everyone."

"I suppose you didn't. I could tell you had a crush on him when we were dating."

"I did," I proudly admitted. "But we aren't talking about me."

"We should."

"Why?"

"Ever since you entered the picture, my life has been turned upside down. You are perfect. At least, my son and ex-husband think you are. Do you know how it kills me when Josh goes on and on about you at home? And now he calls you Mom. And if it wasn't for you, Ryan would probably let me take Josh out of the country." She burst out into tears. "Now I have to make a choice."

"Did Maxime ask you to marry him?"

"Yes."

I did something I never thought I would. I took her hand. At first she flinched, but she allowed me to keep it, though she kept it almost flat. I pulled her off to the side. I didn't give her a choice but to look me in the eye. "First of all, Josh talks about you just as much to us. He loves you, even if you make him eat mango chia whatever for dessert."

Her lip twitched.

"But like it or not, I'm part of his life. I love him. I love his father. I will be the mother of his siblings. I'm a mom to him, but I will never be his mommy. That's all you."

She used her free hand to wipe her eyes. "But I'm not as fun as you."

"So change that. If you need permission to not be perfect, here it is. Life is messy; there's no room for being perfect. But, Victoria, you need to think long and hard about what a life with Maxime will be like, a life with less time with Josh. Because you're right, Ryan won't change the custody agreement. Is Maxime the kind of man you want helping us raise Josh? Does he even want to?"

"He said for me he would try."

"Try?"

"I love him."

"Then I guess you have a choice to make. But before you do, look in the mirror and ask yourself if this is what love looks like. Look at Josh. Don't do something you'll regret just because you think Maxime fits some ideal for you. I would like to think your ideal person would love Josh too, and his proposal wouldn't have you running off crying."

"I don't know what to do," she admitted.

"I think you'll figure it out." At least, I hoped she would. This news was going to kill my husband and break my heart. And what about Josh?

"I know this is gutsy of me to ask, but may I stay? I need to be with Josh. I'll get my own room."

"Yeah, about that." I was going to kill Jay for taking the last available room. "We'd better talk to Ryan."

Seventeen

HERE'S AN UPDATE ON MY vacation. Guess who had to stay? Yep, ex-wife.

It wasn't enough that we were all there together; now, thanks to a snowstorm, we couldn't leave. Thankfully, the Lawtons, including Maviny and Krissy's family had all made it up the mountain before the blizzard hit and they closed I-70. But that meant that Victoria, who really wasn't going anywhere anyway, couldn't leave.

And just like the Christmas story in the Bible, there were no rooms at any inn, hotel, resort, motel, cabin, you name it. My husband checked. So now, his ex-wife was going to be sleeping on our couch. Josh would be joining her, which you'd think would have been somewhat good news to Ryan, but he was too upset and stressed about Maxime and Victoria to even think about sex. Believe me, that was saying something.

The moms, specifically my mom, was causing another set of problems. She was doing her best to stay out of the way, but her presence loomed, and Celia was on the warpath. Both Felicity and Celia were accusing my dad of still being in love with his ex-wife. Celia went a step further and was doing her best to convince Felicity this was the reason why my dad refused to have children with her. So now Felicity was in Celia's room bawling, and Dad was on the verge of calling off the whole wedding. He was done being Celia's punching bag, and he wasn't going to marry anyone who didn't trust him. I couldn't say I blamed him. He hit the gym, trying to burn off steam.

We can't forget about the other mom, Kaye. Guy called Ryan, because Ryan needed more to worry about than his ex-wife marrying a man that from all we had observed would not love our little man. Ryan mentioned that little factoid to Victoria, and she flew off the handle and brought up taking him back to court. Did I mention she was staying in our room?

But I digress. Guy hadn't heard a word from Kaye since she'd arrived in Colorado, and he wanted to check on her. Ryan had had it with the secrets and demanded his dad tell him what was going on. Guy admitted that he'd gone back on his promise to Kaye to retire in March. He never filed his retirement papers, and to top it off, he took this assignment over Christmas. When Ryan asked him why, he explained that he wasn't ready. He felt like it would age him. He took the assignment to prove he could still run with the young bucks, as he called them. Kaye felt betrayed and lied to. She had plans, lots of plans, including getting out of D.C. and moving back to Colorado to be near us. She was ready to go into full grandma mode.

Unmet expectations. It's a killer every time.

Speaking of unmet expectations, Maviny arrived to find Jay had come to surprise her.

See, I expected this to go over smashingly. It was adorable and romantic.

Yeah, Maviny didn't see it that way. She was livid that all she got from him the last several days was a text saying he was alive and not to worry. The way she saw it was that if he didn't know right away that she was what he wanted, it didn't count. Jay came to me seeking advice, but I had none. I was done.

My vacation was a bust. I felt like crap and had been doing my best to act like I didn't feel like death, and all that did was make me more tired.

And here this was supposed to be a happy time. A wedding, Christmas, and a baby. My baby. I didn't want to bring my baby into this mess. I didn't even want to tell Ryan about the beautiful secret I carried under these circumstances. That's when I knew I had to do something. Everyone in my life was going to be deliriously happy, whether they wanted to be or not. I was done messing around. I needed a freaking long winter's nap and some peace, and dang it if I wasn't going to get it.

I booked the corporate room at the restaurant for dinner that night and told everyone that if they weren't there I would personally drag them there. I didn't have the time or energy to talk to each party with problems individually. This was going to be one big group therapy session with food. Besides, I was counting on the fact that since it was in a public setting everyone would behave.

Krissy and Chance and Lawtons, minus Maviny, were easy to convince; they hadn't been fully clued in on all the drama. I think the Lawtons and Krissy and Chance thought they were going to get a good show, so they were excited. I hadn't even had a chance to fill Krissy in on the whole Victoria thing yet, or my mom.

My mother was not invited. I charged her with staying away and taking care of Josh. My big guy didn't need to be a witness to the crazy people that were his relatives. There would be plenty of time for him to figure out the humans in his life were somewhat messed up.

Guy was coming via phone.

Celia at first flat-out refused, but I told her to quit making everything about her, and if she cared at all about her daughter's happiness she would be there. Jury was still out to see if she would show up.

Felicity's brothers and sisters were in, but I think for the same reasons as the Lawtons and Krissy and Chance—they wanted a show. I was sure Eden and Candy were hoping for me to stand up to Celia again. It was a dirty job, but somebody had to do it.

That left dear, dear, dear Victoria. I thought if I said dear enough, I might believe she was. Nope. I didn't hate her. Part of me felt bad for her. She obviously loved Maxime, and she had some messed-up views about life that made her act like she'd eaten peed-on Cheerios every morning. But if she thought we were going to let Josh move to France with a man who had no intention of being a good father figure without a fight, she was crazy.

When Ryan and I were dating, Josh was his priority. Every decision he made was based on what was best for Josh. Victoria owed it to Josh and Ryan to do the same thing now, and forever, for that matter. I told her the same, and that I expected her to come. It was the least she could do for crashing our vacation.

By showtime, I was dead on my feet. I had only eaten a handful of pretzels and a few sips of ginger ale.

The corporate room had one large table and several smaller ones around the perimeter of the room. I made everyone sit at the large table and gave them seating assignments. I meant business. We were adults, and I refused to let anyone be a petulant child. We all had excellent vocabulary skills, and we were going to use them. It was amazing what actual talking could do to solve problems.

The dynamics around the table were interesting. You had the one half all smiles and eager to see some action. The other half was tense, like you needed a chainsaw to cut through the bad vibes.

I decided eating first was best, well, at least for everyone but me. I didn't need any hangry people. Several servers came in and took everyone's orders. I noticed there was a lot of alcohol being ordered by the brooding half. Even my Ryan, who rarely drank, ordered a beer. Victoria needed one of their special, no-taste menus. Honestly, if she just ate a cookie or something she would probably like life a lot more.

I had the pleasure of sitting between Ryan and his ex and across from Felicity, Dad, and Celia. I needed to keep my eye on them. Felicity and Dad were barely speaking, and Celia kept throwing me dirty looks. Like I said before, she had nothing on Victoria and didn't scare me. Kaye held her phone in her hand, waiting for Guy to call, but if she gripped it any tighter she was going to obliterate it.

Maviny and Jay were seated next to each other, and I watched Jay do his best to engage Maviny in discussion. He was even trying to be cute with her and play with her hair or whisper in her ear, but she wasn't having it and kept pushing him away. She was being ridiculous. I would tell her soon. But food first.

My only saving grace was Krissy, who kept texting me funny emojis to describe what only could be described as insanity. My favorites were the volcano waiting to explode and the poop one. That pretty much summed it up.

The conversation before dinner arrived was like one big weather forecast. Really? That's all we could talk about was the weather? It was snowing. Big deal. We lived in Colorado, and it was December in the mountains. Snow was a given. But this conversation was better than what was to come. It was the calm before the real storm. The blizzard had nothing on the dumping and frigid temps that hit the room as soon as dinner was served.

We can thank the server for bringing Celia the wrong dish. That's all it took for the floodgates to open.

"Can you people get anything right here? I told you no cilantro."

"Do you have to complain about everything?" My dad had had enough.

I couldn't fault him, but Felicity could.

"Don't talk to my mother that way."

Dad gave Felicity the coldest stare. I didn't even know he could look like that. Not even when I wrecked his car when I was sixteen did he look like that.

That wasn't the only drama that ensued. Wouldn't you

know it, Victoria agreed with Celia. They were two peed-on Cheerios in a pod. "I hate when they don't bring you the correct order."

"You hate everything." Ryan jumped into the fray.

You'd never seen servers at a restaurant move so fast. They all closed the door behind them and ran. If I'd had the energy, I would have too. Instead I watched the war of words around the table. Except for the few who were shoveling food into their mouths like they were eating popcorn watching a show.

Kaye was on the phone yelling at Guy about something he had done in 1991. Maviny and Jay were going at it, causing Taylar Ann to cry. She was next to them on Chance's lap. Chance used it as his out and hightailed it out of there with his baby. Krissy stayed to enjoy the show; she was even snapping pictures. Ann and Ken Lawton were in shock. They were actually my "couple" hero. They gave me hope relationships lasted.

It got so bad, mild-mannered Jay was standing up and ready to go. My dad was two millimeters away from calling off the wedding. Kaye informed Guy she was never coming home. And Ryan and Victoria were throwing their lawyers' names around and threatening to see each other in court.

I couldn't take it one more second. With every ounce of energy I had left, I stood up, stars in my eyes and all. I had to hold on to the table for support. Ryan didn't even notice, and I was standing between him and Victoria, who had tears streaming down her face.

"Enough!" I leaned against the table.

Silence instantaneously reigned.

I took some shallow breaths because I felt like if I breathed too deep I would either puke or pass out. One or the other might happen either way.

"Listen to me." I scanned the table and glared at everyone, even my husband, whose head looked ready to explode. "This is not how family behaves. We all came up here to celebrate love; instead you've all done your best to destroy it."

I set my sights on Felicity and Dad. "Felicity, I love you. My dad loves only you. He has been nothing but honest with you about his feelings and where he is in his life and where he would like to go. If you can't accept that or trust him, then you shouldn't marry him. You both deserve to be with someone who accepts where you're at."

I wasn't so nice to Celia. "Celia, you need to accept your daughter's choices whether you agree with them or not. She's an adult. And lay off my dad. You'll never find a better man for your daughter."

I saw Candy and Eden from the corner of my eye quietly applauding me.

"Well." Celia threw her napkin on her plate but didn't say another word.

Felicity and Dad turned to each other but didn't speak, at least not in words. Their eyes seemed to be communicating. I couldn't tell exactly what they were saying, but the anger was gone.

Next, I set my sights on Maviny and Jay. "Maviny, just be honest with Jay. Passive aggressive doesn't look good on anyone. The man came up here to surprise you, and you've done your best to ruin what could be a great story to tell one day. So he got a little scared. Don't hold that against him."

Maviny smirked at me before throwing her arms around Jay.

Kaye must have known she was next. She put Guy on speaker.

"Mom and Dad, I don't know exactly what's going on, but keeping secrets and running away never solved a thing. Dad, if you're scared, be honest with Mom. And if it's getting old you're afraid of, I know a little boy who would love to have his grandpa around more and could help keep you young." Guy chuckled over the phone, and Kaye wiped a tear out of her eye.

I was barely standing at this point, but Ryan and especially Victoria needed to hear me out. Victoria dared me with her gorgeous, blurry blue eyes to say anything to her.

I loved a good challenge. She should know that about me by now.

"Ryan and I recognize we have no say in who you marry."

Victoria gave me a you-got-that-right look.

"But remember when you told me you were lucky that Ryan found a woman who treated your son well and loved him?"

Her eyes and chin dipped.

"That's all Ryan and I want in return. A man for you who will love Josh and you the way you both deserve. You know I have no love for you."

Oh my gosh, she smiled at me.

"But this I will give you, you're a good mother. Will you really be happy with a man who isn't a good father?"

"Please think about this." Ryan pleaded with her.

Victoria said nothing, but I saw in her eyes that she was listening.

My work was done. I was done. My eyes filled with stars before I collapsed.

Good thing Ryan had good reflexes. He caught me before I hit the solid wood chair or hard floor.

"Charlee!" ten people must have said, but it was Ryan's voice I focused on.

Ryan easily picked me up, just like that one night I accidentally drank a whole bunch of what I thought were virgin daiquiris, but they ended up being the real deal. I thought I was going to die that night, I felt so bad. This was worse.

Leave it to someone to panic. I wasn't sure who it was, but I heard the words, "Should I dial 911?"

No! I wanted to scream. "I'm fine," I managed to get out.

"Charlee, you're not fine." My husband had to be paler than me with worry.

The moms of the room had to get involved. Kaye, Ann, and Felicity shrouded around us.

Dad was pushing his way through. "I told you, Ryan, something was wrong." He didn't sound happy with my husband.

Ryan paid no one else any attention but me. "I'm taking you to the clinic."

I tried to shake my head, but nothing was working right, and if I moved I felt like I would puke.

"Yes, yes, yes," all the moms agreed with Ryan.

"Baby girl, hang in there." I swore my dad was in tears.

"I'm not dying. I'm pregnant, for crying out loud." That was so not how I wanted that to go down, but at least the panicked people calmed the heck down. I peered into my husband's tear-filled eyes. "Merry Christmas."

He held me closer and kissed my lips.

I think there was some celebrating going on around me, but I was in my favorite place, Ryan World.

"You're still going to the clinic."

"Oh, fine."

Eighteen

THE WEDDING WAS STILL ON, and I was feeling better after my night in urgent care being treated for dehydration and a day of rest yesterday. I wanted to kiss the doctor for whatever anti-nausea medicine he placed in my IV. It was the best I had felt in weeks.

Maybe I should have announced I was pregnant earlier. It was like a magic wand. For this new life, everyone wanted to get along. Baby JC made them remember what was most important. It didn't hurt that everyone was waiting on me hand and foot. Score. Well, not Victoria, but at least she wasn't giving me peed-on-Cheerio looks. She was actually pretty depressed. She didn't accept Maxime's proposal, to the great relief of Ryan and myself. She mainly moped around the suite, even though we invited her to the wedding and all the activities surrounding it.

Maviny and Jay announced that Jay was going to go to Ireland with Maviny. Guy and Kaye were going to meet in Germany after Christmas, so maybe Guy didn't really work for the CIA. I don't think she would be allowed to go on any missions. I was kind of bummed by that. Mom was

155

already shopping for the baby and undecided about her own marriage. Felicity and Dad, like I said, were still getting married and were acting like it. Save it for the honeymoon, please, I wanted to say, but I preferred it over their bickering any day.

But no one, except maybe Ryan, was happier about my news than Josh. He had asked Santa for a baby brother or sister, mostly a brother, but if he had to, he would take a sister. Whew. So happy he wasn't going to be disappointed with his laser tag come Christmas morning.

Since the news broke, Ryan followed me around everywhere. If he wasn't putting his hand on my abdomen, he was kissing it or me. I wasn't complaining. I couldn't even get ready for the wedding without him. No, really, I couldn't. I needed help zipping up my deep-green evening gown, and Ryan was happy to oblige.

"I like it better when the zipper goes the other way." He kissed the nape of my neck.

The butterflies applauded. That was one of their favorite spots. "You'll get your chance, don't worry."

His beautiful eyes met mine in the bathroom mirror we were standing in front of getting all spiffy. They held a mischievous glint to them.

"You know, I knew you were pregnant."

"How?"

He brushed my curled hair to the side and kissed his way up my neck. In between kisses he said, "I haven't been on a tampon run in weeks."

I laughed. "That doesn't prove anything. I could have planned ahead and bought my own."

"And when has that happened since we've been together?"

"Good point." He'd been buying me tampons since before we were engaged. It was how I knew he was a keeper.

"I do have other proof, though."

"Is that so?" I smiled at him through the mirror.

Tragically, his lips and hands departed from my body. He reached into his suit coat. I should mention he looked like fire in his black suit and silver tie. He pulled out the flat, envelope-looking gift that had been under our tree and handed it to me. "Merry Christmas, Charlee."

"I thought we were waiting to open gifts until tomorrow?"

"With our extra visitors, I wanted to give you this in private."

I turned around and took the gift. I gently tore at the red paper. The gift felt so light I didn't want to damage anything. Inside I found a handwritten letter. I dropped the wrapping paper but kept the letter and unfolded it. I recognized Ryan's scribbles right away.

Dear Beautiful Wife and Mother-to-Be,

My eyes flew up and caught Ryan's smiling ones. Tears filled my own.

"Keep reading." Ryan was enjoying this.

This has been the best year of my life, but I know the best is yet to come. August, right?

I put my hand to my mouth and laughed. He sure knew how to calculate a due date.

Before diapers and never-ending midnight feedings

become the norm, I've booked a trip for just you and me to Saint Lucia in February to celebrate the anniversary of the smartest thing I ever did, asking you to be my wife.

Merry Christmas.

All my love,

Ryan

P.S. Did you really think I would only spend $100 on you?

I dropped the letter and wrapped my arms around his neck. "If you knew I was pregnant, why didn't you say something? And why did you keep asking me to do things you knew a pregnant woman shouldn't do?"

"Because I enjoyed the excuses you kept coming up with, and I was hoping I could get you to tell me."

I kissed his cheek. "By the way, my gift is still better than yours, but this comes in at a close second. Thank you."

He laughed before his lips crashed onto mine, making the butterflies beg for us to be late to the wedding. I wanted to give them and Ryan their way, but duty called.

WE STOOD IN THE SILVER- and green-draped resort wedding hall, surrounded by family and friends, to watch Dad and Felicity finally tie the knot. Who knew it would be so much trouble getting them there? But by the look of contentment on my dad's face when Felicity walked down the aisle escorted by her brothers, it was well worth it.

While the preacher read their vows, I stared at my

handsome husband, who was the best man, and my big guy, the ring bearer, standing across from me. Such love filled me. And despite the craziness, I got my Christmas wish. I really had it all along. Ryan and Josh and the little one I carried were the best gifts I could ever ask for.

Except maybe that long winter's nap.

Epilogue

"SHE'S SO BEAUTIFUL, JUST LIKE her mother." Ryan couldn't keep his eyes off his daughter with matted-down, brown hair and skin as soft as fleece.

I kissed the head of the tiny package of joy in his arms. "Don't you think he looks like Josh?"

Ryan took his eyes off Elizabeth and smiled down on Alexander. Didn't I tell you Ryan had a thing for stuffy names? I would be calling them Lizzy and Al.

"They have the same nose." Ryan snuggled Al.

I leaned my head against Ryan's shoulder. I was exhausted. Those first few months of tired had nothing on twelve hours of labor. I thought I was going to die, but now, lying in the hospital bed with the man I was cursing yesterday and swearing I would never have sex with again, I was happier than I had ever been. Two perfect babies, weighing close to six pounds each and who had sucked the life out of me, had arrived healthy two weeks before their due date. They came not a moment too soon. I was as big as a house.

Josh came flying through the hospital room door

with the grandparent brigade and startled his sister and brother. Two of the saddest sounds escaped our precious bundles.

Josh jumped on the bed and kissed them both. "Don't cry. I brought you stuffed animals."

The babies didn't really care for the cute pink and blue bears their big brother was trying to shove in their faces. For little things, they had some great lungs.

My newly single mom, dad, Felicity, Guy, and Kaye all stood there enjoying the scene, the new chaos that would be our life.

Josh plugged his ears. "Make them stop!"

Ryan and I bounced and tried to soothe our babies, but they seemed to feed off each other. It was like a contest to see who could cry the loudest. I think Lizzy was edging out Al.

A look passed between Ryan and me, and reality hit us.

We were in trouble. Lots and lots of trouble.

If you enjoyed *More Trouble in Loveland*, here are some other books by Jennifer Peel that you may enjoy:

Merry Little Hate Notes
The Spy Who Ghosted Me
The Proximity Factor
Forgettable in Every Way
The Valentine Inn
All's Fair in Love and Business
My eX-MAS Emergency
The Holiday Ex-Files
My Not So Wicked Stepbrother
Facial Recognition
The Sidelined Wife
How to Get Over Your Ex in Ninety Days
Narcissistic Tendencies
Trouble in Loveland
Paige's Turn

For a complete list of all her books,
visit her Amazon page.

Jennifer Peel is a *USA Today* best-selling author who didn't grow up wanting to be a writer—she was aiming for something more realistic, like being the first female president. When that didn't work out, she started writing just before her fortieth birthday. Now, after publishing several award-winning and best-selling novels, she's addicted to typing and chocolate. When she's not glued to her laptop and a bag of Dove dark chocolates, she loves spending time with her family, making daily Target runs, reading, and pretending she can do Zumba.

***

If you enjoyed this book, please rate and review it.
You can also connect with Jennifer on social media or join her Facebook readers group, Jen's Book Besties:
Facebook
Instagram
Jen's Book Besties

To learn more about Jennifer and her books, visit her website at www.jenniferpeel.com.